Jason, Julia and Rick know Argo
Manor is hiding a secret – and they're
going to unravel the mystery.

No matter what the consequences. . .

Look out for...

Ulysses Moore and the Long-lost Map

ULYSSES MOORE

THE DOOR TO TIME

WITHDRAWN FROM STOCK

■SCHOLASTIC

First published in the UK in 2007 by Scholastic Children's Books
An imprint of Scholastic Ltd
Euston House, 24 Eversholt Street
London, NW1 1DB, UK
Registered office: Westfield Road, Southam, Warwickshire, CV47 0RA
SCHOLASTIC and associated logos are trademarks and/or registered trademarks of
Scholastic Inc.

First published in the US by Scholastic Inc., 2006
Text copyright © 2004 by Edizioni Piemme S.p.A., via Galeotto del Carretto 10, 15033
Casale Monferrato (AL) Italia. English translation © 2006 by Edizioni Piemme S.p.A.
Ulysses Moore names, characters, and related indicia are coyright, trademark, and
exclusive licence of Edizioni Piemme S.p.A

Text by Pierodomenico Baccalario. Original title: *La Porta del Tempo*.
Original illustrations by Iacopo Bruno. Graphics by Iacopo Bruno and Laura Zuccotti
Translation by Leah Janeczko. Special thanks to James Preller. Editorial project by
Marcella Drago and Clare Stringer

The right of Pierodomenico Baccalario to be identified as the author
of this work has been asserted by him.
Cover illustration by Adam Stower, 2007

10 digit ISBN 0 439 95015 5
13 digit ISBN 978 0439 95015 2

British Library Cataloguing-in-Publication Data.
A CIP catalogue record for this book is available from the British Library
All rights reserved
This book is sold subject to the condition that it shall not, by way of trade or otherwise,
be lent, hired out or otherwise circulated in any form of binding or cover other than
that in which it is published. No part of this publication may be reproduced, stored in
a retrieval system, or transmitted in any form or by any means (electronic, mechanical,
photocopying, recording or otherwise) without the prior written permission of
Scholastic Limited.

Printed by CPI Bookmarque, Croydon, Surrey
Papers used by Scholastic Children's Books are made from wood grown in
sustainable forests.

1 3 5 7 9 10 8 6 4 2

This is a work of fiction. Names, characters, places, incidents and dialogues are products
of the author's imagination or are used fictitiously. Any resemblance to actual people,
living or dead, events or locales is entirely coincidental.

www.scholastic.co.uk/zone

Contents

Dear Reader

Last July, we received the following email from one of our editors, Michael Merryweather. Once we read it, we knew we had to share this story with you immediately. Michael has been in Cornwall since then, searching for other lost manuscripts written by the mysterious Ulysses Moore.

Thank you for joining us on this adventure – we have no idea where it will end up!

Your friends at
Scholastic

From: Michael Merryweather
Date: 20 July, 2006 03:48
To: The editors at Scholastic Ltd
Subject: A fascinating mystery

▼ Attachments:

🖼 trunk.jpg	56 K	Open
🖼 map.jpg	181 K	Save
		Remove

I know you all thought I was crazy, going to Cornwall to search for Ulysses Moore and his manuscripts. But I am on to something. I'm sure of it. I am now in the town of Zennor, because I can't find Kilmore Cove (where Ulysses is said to live) on the map. I'm not sure it even exists.

There is grave danger here. I've asked many people about Ulysses – their faces just go white. Then today, I found a trunk at my door. And inside was a manuscript written by Ulysses Moore himself! It's in some sort of code, but I'm slowly working out how to translate it. The manuscript tells the story of three children who stumble upon something very powerful . . . and maybe dangerous. I am fascinated.

Once I finish this translation, I urge you to get this out to the children of Britain. We need their help in order to solve this mystery. Who *is* Ulysses Moore?

There are more manuscripts out there. I just know it.

I must go. I will write or call again soon.

MM

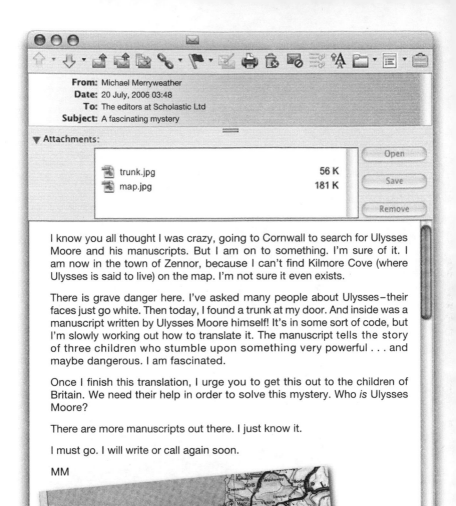

THE DOOR TO TIME

Ulysses Moore

~ 1 ~

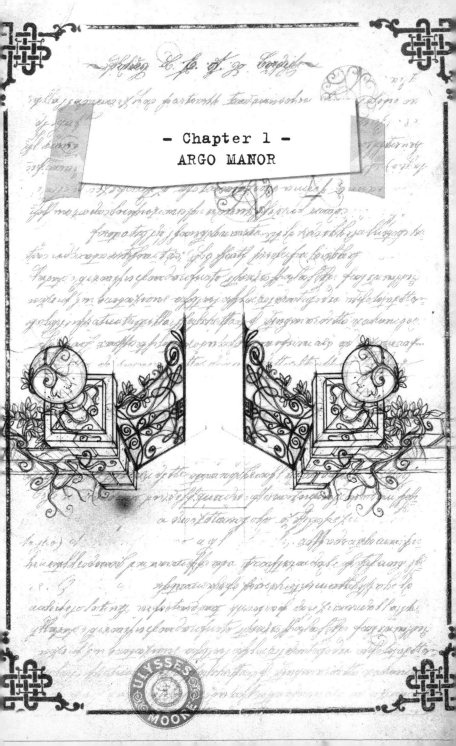

– Chapter 1 –
ARGO MANOR

The house appeared suddenly from around the bend. Its stone tower rose up like a finger pointing at the sky. It was framed by the grey-blue sea.

"Wow," gasped Mrs Covenant.

Behind the wheel, her husband simply smiled. He steered the car through a forbidding iron gate – open specifically for their arrival, he guessed – and parked the car in the courtyard.

Mrs Covenant got out, the white gravel crunching beneath her feet. She blinked and stared, touching her fingers to her lips as if she was not yet sure that she could believe her eyes.

The house was perched high upon a cliff overlooking the sea. Waves crashed against the rocks far below. The air had a sharp, salty taste. The house was enclosed by the blue of the sea and sky as if it were about to be swallowed up by nature herself. Tidy rows of trees stood at each side, punctuated by flowers of every colour. From the edge of the cliff, a visitor could just glimpse a small sandy beach below. Further out was the bay of Kilmore Cove. A town had gathered around it, its houses huddled close to the sea. Every house, every person, the entire town – it all centred around the lure of the sea.

As she stood in the courtyard, eyes blinking with

amazement, Mrs Covenant was joined by an old man, his face covered with deep wrinkles and a trim white beard.

The man's gaze was intense, searching. "My name is Nestor," he said. "I'm the caretaker here at Argo Manor."

So that's the name: Argo Manor. How strange, Mrs Covenant thought. Meanwhile, the caretaker had started limping in the direction of the house. He led the couple to an ornate porch that offered a breathtaking view of the sea below.

"Are you sure we're not mistaken?" Mrs Covenant asked in disbelief. She brushed her hand along the walls of Argo Manor as if to reassure herself that it was real, that this wasn't all some fantastic dream.

Her husband took her hand. His wife's reaction to this place delighted him. She was already overwhelmed. And they hadn't even stepped inside! "Now get ready for this," he whispered in her ear.

The inside of Argo Manor was even more spectacular than the outside. Nestor swept them off on a hurried tour of the house, darting in and out of rooms, opening doors, pulling back curtains, then quickly ushering the Covenants along to the next room. The house wasn't just old, it had . . . *personality*. Yes, that was the word, thought Mrs Covenant. Personality, as if it were a living thing instead of a mere house of stone and wood. The furniture was a crazy jumble of styles, seemingly from every corner of the globe: an Egyptian vase, a Venetian desk, Persian rugs, a painting from the Hudson River School. Yet somehow it all worked. Everything had its place.

"Tell me this is all true," Mrs Covenant murmured to her husband. "This is all ours? Tell me I'm not dreaming."

He squeezed her hand. "It's true, my dear," he replied. "Welcome to your new home."

The caretaker led them through a small archway into an elegant sitting room that had an ancient ceiling with exposed beams. The walls were stone. Across the room there was another door – a door of dark wood set into the far wall.

"This is one of the oldest rooms," Nestor said. He smiled with satisfaction. "The former owner, Mr Ulysses Moore, was very strict about certain details. He insisted that these rooms stay true to their original function. But time changes all. There once was a medieval tower here that was destroyed by a storm long ago. The only change that Mr Moore allowed to this room was to seal off the draughty windows and, naturally, to have electrical wiring installed. Though, I confess," he added, "we still have problems with the draught."

"Jason will love it here," Mr Covenant said.

His wife remained silent. Her thoughts were on her daughter, Julia.

"There are two children, isn't that right?" the caretaker inquired.

"Yes. A boy and a girl, both eleven years old," Mrs Covenant replied. "Twins."

Nestor's eyes twinkled. "And I imagine they're

bright, and full of life! How happy they will be here," he said. "Don't worry about them, madam. The house may be isolated, but it contains a world of excitement for the young and adventurous."

"Oh, they're adventurous, all right," Mrs Convenant said with a smile. She was not worried about Jason. He was a dreamer, and she knew that he'd instantly feel the magic of this place. But Julia was different. She was a city girl who enjoyed the buzz and bounce of urban living: the noises, the mad rush, the whirlwind of faces and culture.

Mr Covenant seemed to read his wife's thoughts. "They'll be fine," he said reassuringly. "Even Julia. It'll be good for them both."

Mrs Covenant nodded. "Yes, of course," she told Nestor. "The twins will be thrilled."

"Perfect," purred Nestor, stroking his beard. "Just perfect. So it's a deal then?" He thrust out his hand to Mr Covenant.

Mr Covenant explained to his wife that the former owner, Ulysses Moore, was an eccentric; an old man with peculiar ideas. He had wished for the house to be leased only to a young family with at least two children.

Nestor nodded in agreement. "He wanted the house to be full of life," the caretaker explained.

"Old Mr Moore believed that a house without young voices was like a man who was dead."

He led the couple back outside. A moment before she walked out, something made Mrs Covenant pause under the archway. She turned to look again at the door in the eastern wall. The wood looked burnt in some places, as if it had survived a fire. In other places, it was scarred by scrapes and deep gashes. As if – could it be? – someone had once taken an axe to it in a fit of rage.

"What happened to that door?" she asked.

Nestor stopped, glanced from the door to Mrs Covenant, and shook his head.

"Ah, I'm sorry," he replied. "Mr Moore's orders. That door should have been replaced long ago. Just pretend it isn't there." He walked to the door, crossed his arms, and eyed it like an old adversary. "It has been through everything, this old door. Long ago the keys to open it were, um, misplaced. You see these four holes? Mr Moore believed they were locks. He tried to open it in every imaginable way, but it was no use. This door," Nestor concluded, "is sealed for ever."

"And where did it lead?" wondered Mr Covenant.

The caretaker shrugged. "Who knows? It's a

mystery to me. This old house is full of secrets. Once this door might have provided a short cut to the old water tank, but even that no longer exists." He gazed at the door thoughtfully. "It's a door without a purpose."

Mrs Covenant ran her hand gently down the blackened, scratched wood and felt a pang of concern. "Maybe we should put something in front of it," she said, turning to her husband. "I wouldn't want the children to try to open it."

"Excellent idea," Nestor quickly agreed, limping out of the room. "That's the best thing to do. The children should never get it in their minds to try to open it."

- Chapter 2 -
FOOTSTEPS

Dr. Clifton

The GUIDE
to
PARANORMAL
CREATURES

Jason Covenant stood perfectly still at the bottom of the stairs, listening intently. There was a strange draught, a breeze carrying distant noises – the creaking of the furniture, the murmuring of the wind, the scampering of small feet.

In the last few days, Jason had imagined that the furniture at Argo Manor had a life of its own. As soon as you left the room, it moved a millimetre. Just a millimetre and no more, so that it wouldn't be caught doing it. Could such a thing be possible?

But this time it was different. It couldn't have been a piece of furniture that had moved. Or the seagulls perched on the tiled roof, the lizards in the ivy or the mice in the attic. No.

This time he had heard a distinct sound: hurried footsteps coming from the floor above. Jason had stopped dead in his tracks to listen, barely breathing, and he heard the footsteps once again.

Jason frowned, worried. "Then you're upstairs," he murmured to the mysterious intruder. It was as though there was some sort of challenge between them. A contest of wills.

How could it be that no one else in his family had noticed it? How could it be that neither his father, nor his mother, or even his sister, Julia, had understood that there was someone else in that enormous house? Why did the voices speak to him and only him?

Jason had understood it instantly, from the first moment he set his suitcases down in the courtyard. There was something here: a mysterious presence, a force, a mystery of some kind. Argo Manor was far too large a house for Jason to know every bit of it. It was a house of rooms and secrets, a house with a history. A house that had witnessed strange things. No one had to tell Jason. He knew it – no, that wasn't it – he *felt* it as if it were a physical sensation, the way a person shivers in the cold or pulls a hand away from a fire. Somehow, Jason felt things that others didn't. It was his gift, his strangeness. All his life it had been true. His body just *knew* things sometimes.

When they'd faced each other for the first time, it was as though Argo Manor had whispered to him, "Not everything is as it seems. Come and discover my secret, Jason!"

And he had accepted the challenge.

Standing in the draught, Jason looked up at the portraits hanging on the wall that flanked the staircase leading to the first floor and then up to the tower room, where the stairs ended at a mirrored door. His father had explained that the framed portraits were those of the former owners of the house, and promised that one day their own portraits would hang beside the others.

"Oh, no way. I'm not posing for *that*," had been Julia's immediate reply. She cringed at the very thought. "I'm not going to sit around and have some crazy painter turn me into a zombie-looking dork. Get real."

But Jason liked the idea. It would make him feel like an important person. Like a part of history.

"I know you're here," Jason whispered now. He wondered: could the footsteps he'd heard belong to a ghost? Do ghosts even *have* footsteps?

Jason reached into his pocket and pulled out his *Guide to Paranormal Creatures*, written by the famous cult hero, Dr Harold Rawlings Clifton. Jason had seen his special on TV. He had surfed the websites. Now he had Dr Clifton's latest book.

Jason quickly found the page he was looking for. "*Do not be led to believe that ghosts are silent. They can make noises of all kinds (footsteps, jangling chains, ringing bells) and often can speak. What is more, they are not always without bodies,*" he read aloud.

Jason nodded and took heart. These few lines confirmed his suspicion about the strange presence in this house. And they also resolved something that had confused him terribly. He had always wondered why, in the movies, ghosts walked through doors and never, for instance, through floors.

He continued reading. *"Ghosts normally haunt homes in which there is something unresolved that must be completed."*

Something unresolved. Of course. That must be the solution. It might be a ghost that was roaming the first floor in order to complete, well, to complete . . . *something.*

Jason quickly reread Dr Clifton's advice on how to find a ghost. Then he slipped the book into his back pocket. "Now the hunter becomes the hunted. Look out, ghost. I'm coming after *you!*"

But the instant he rested his foot on the first step, a hand grabbed him from behind.

"Hey, Jason!" shouted Julia. "Haven't you heard us calling? Come on!"

Still lost in thought, Jason didn't have a clue what his sister was talking about. *We have to go?* he asked himself. *Now? Where?*

Nothing came to mind, but he knew it would be impossible to stay here and try to convince Julia that there was a ghost on the first floor. Julia wasn't like that. She didn't believe in anything she couldn't taste, touch, or buy with her father's credit card. Julia did believe in some things. Like expensive things. She had no interest in ghosts.

Jason followed his twin sister into the courtyard.

He suddenly remembered what was in store for the afternoon. His parents were going to London to oversee the final details of their move. There was still some furniture to be packed up, files to organize, bank accounts to be transferred, his mother's art studio to bring back, and endless other details to see to. Fortunately, Jason and Julia would be spared the boredom. Their parents would return to Argo Manor on Sunday morning with a removal van. Meanwhile, the twins were to stay at the manor under the supervision of the caretaker, Mr Nestor.

They had got permission to invite over Rick Banner, a boy from town whom they had recently met at school, so maybe they wouldn't be too bored. Rick was their first friend in Kilmore Cove, and he seemed to know everything about the town.

The twins walked to the family car. Sunlight speckled the courtyard, filtered through tall trees and scattering clouds. In the distance, on the horizon of the sea, a thin white line seemed to separate sky from water.

"Have you ever wondered why the sky turns white before it touches the sea?" Jason asked his sister.

"Nope," replied Julia. "But I have wondered when you'll ever learn how to use a comb." She reached up to rearrange a few loose strands of hair. "Hopeless," Julia muttered, but not unkindly.

Just before they reached the car, Jason whirled around to stare up at the first floor windows. He was sure that he'd manage to surprise the ghost and catch it gazing through the panes. But it was too quick. Jason saw nothing at all.

Nestor listened impatiently to Mrs Covenant's detailed instructions. When she had counted up to number eight on her fingers, he interrupted her.

MR. ULYSSES MOORE
ARGO MANOR
1 SALTON CLIFF
KILMORE COVE
CORNWALL
TR 26 3BY
Jason and Julia Covenant (UK)

"Madam, if you will permit me," he said, raising a hand. "I am not a babysitter. And I do not think your children need one. Everything will be fine. Please, don't worry."

In the car, Mr Covenant tapped lightly on the horn. He was in a hurry to leave. This only annoyed his wife. She refused to be rushed, especially where the safety and well-being of her children were concerned. She stood firmly in the driveway, ignoring the horn.

Nestor tried to bring the conversation to a rapid close. "Today Jason and Julia are going to wear themselves out exploring the house with their friend from town. They will swim and run and do whatever it is that children do, and tonight they will be so tired that they will go straight to sleep."

"Yes, but. . ."

Mr Nestor smiled, shaking his head. "You are a good mother. You love your children very much, Mrs Covenant," he said. "But please go. Trust me. Trust Jason and Julia. It is a beautiful day and I have much to do. Jason and Julia will be well cared for, it is my solemn promise. Besides," he added, "there's nothing dangerous at Argo Manor."

Mrs Covenant gestured towards the water. "But the cliff. . ." she began.

The caretaker laughed. "Perhaps we should keep them tucked up in their beds all day? Would you like that? Yes, Mrs Covenant, the world is full of risks and dangers. That is life."

"But you don't know Jason the way I do," Mrs Covenant replied, dropping her voice to a whisper. "If there's trouble around, he'll find it."

Jason and Julia finally joined them. Jason walked backwards, staring dreamily at the house. He tripped over a garden hose and had to spin around quickly to avoid falling flat on the gravel.

"See what I mean?" sighed his mother.

Nestor scratched his white beard. "He is athletic and adventurous?"

Mrs Covenant laughed. "I suppose that's one way of looking at it," she admitted.

Julia threw her arms around her mother's neck. Then she propped herself up on the car door to give her father a kiss. "If you want to bring us back presents," she cooed, "we won't complain!"

Jason simply waved, his thoughts elsewhere.

"Remember, children," called Mrs Covenant as she got into the car, "listen to Nestor and don't do anything silly."

Jason and Julia nodded, smiling. The old caretaker made a wry face.

The car pulled away, leaving in its wake a little spray of gravel. When it reached the gate, Mrs Covenant turned to wave goodbye to her children.

"Are you sure they'll be all right?" she asked her husband.

He just smiled at her and continued driving.

Mrs Covenant sank back into her seat. She was far too overprotective; she knew that. But even so, an uneasy feeling came over her. "I worry," she whispered.

Her husband squeezed her fingers. "That's because you love them so much," he said. "It's OK. They'll be fine. Nestor will take good care of them."

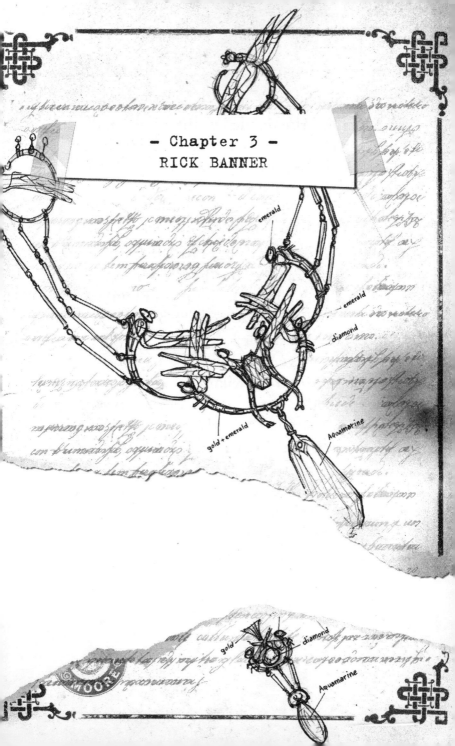

- Chapter 3 -
RICK BANNER

emerald

emerald

diamond

gold + emerald

Aquamarine

gold

diamond

Aquamarine

Rick Banner pedalled steadily up the long, gradual rise that led to the house on the cliff. Sweat soaked his shirt and dripped from his forehead. He was feeling the strain. Every muscle in his body shouted, "Stop!"

But no way. Not Rick. Especially not today. He pushed on.

His calves were burning, a pain that felt like they were literally on fire. But he knew it was a good ache, a healthy burn; it built up your muscles. "If it doesn't kill you," his father used to tell him, "then it only makes you stronger."

And his father knew. He had once bicycled all around Britain, from Kilmore Cove to the Isle of Skye, in Scotland, and back.

So Rick continued to pedal hard, anticipating the moment when he'd find himself in front of the tower that rose up over Argo Manor.

His energy increased. For years Rick had dreamed of visiting that house, of stepping just once inside its towering walls. He had spent hours looking at it through binoculars from the windows of his house or from the beach, at low tide. It was a magical place. A magnet that drew Rick in. And now, finally, miraculously, he was almost there. Its doors were about to open to him.

Just thinking of Argo Manor made Rick's legs feel stronger – loose and well oiled. The great house sat at the top of the granite cliffs, massive walls of rock scoured by salt spray. Sailors called them the Salton Cliffs. All those mysterious stories he'd heard about that house and its eccentric owner who had lived there for forty years, the incredible Ulysses Moore!

Rick allowed his mind to wander back through the days. Only last week, he had introduced himself to Jason and Julia at Kilmore Cove's small school. The new children were from the city, and their sudden presence was felt throughout the school. But

Rick was the first to step up, hold out his hand, and offer friendship.

The twins were a year younger than Rick. They knew nothing about the town, yet they had just moved into the house of his dreams. And Rick would be their guide to the strange new world of Kilmore Cove. Their arrival had offered him an amazing opportunity, and he was ready to take it.

Rick grinned at the sight of Argo Manor's black gates just around the bend. He lifted himself off his seat, shifting into a sprint.

At that moment, he sensed something behind him. He had had the road to himself for the last half-hour, but now a car was quickly approaching. Rick swerved to the slim shoulder of the road. The car's horn blared as it sped past. *Pop!* His rear tyre hit a rock and blew. Rick lost control of the bike and tumbled on to his side, sliding across the hard pavement.

Scraped, bruised, but not seriously hurt, Rick untangled himself from the frame of the bike. He picked himself up at the side of the road and shook his fist at the reckless driver.

The car suddenly screeched to a stop, as if its driver had seen Rick's angry gesture. It was one of those enormous cars with dark tinted windows, the kind you'd see in old gangster movies or pulling up to the red carpet at the Academy Awards.

Uh-oh. Rick gulped and quickly looked away from the car and down at his bike. Some paint was scraped and the spokes looked bent.

A rear window of the car slid down. "Darling, I'm so terribly sorry! Are you all right?" exclaimed a woman's voice.

A slender hand covered with a bright orange glove and glittering with bracelets emerged from the rear window and waved him over.

"I'm sorry, my dear little boy," the woman's voice continued. "Is your bicycle all right?"

Rick decided to ignore the "dear little boy" comment. He drew just close enough to peek inside the car. He saw two long legs, a cascade of red hair, an intricate necklace, and a remarkably beautiful face. The woman's eyes were green and, to Rick, they resembled those of a Persian cat. A sweet cloud of perfume drifted towards him.

"You *must* forgive us," the woman purred, as if she expected forgiveness from all men, even so-called "dear little boys".

"My servant thinks he's a Formula One driver," she continued. "Isn't that right, Manfred? Perhaps you should apologize to our young friend?" There was an air of command to her tone. Beneath the silk in her voice, there was iron. She was a woman who was used to getting her way.

The driver's door opened and Manfred stepped out. He was a burly young man with a brutish face. He wore an elegant pinstriped suit, but it didn't seem to fit him properly. He bowed stiffly and mumbled an insincere apology. He reached into his jacket pocket and produced a wad of money. "This should cover the cost of repairs."

"Very well, Manfred," the woman called from the back seat. "Things to do, places to go," she murmured. Then louder, to Rick, "A thousand pardons, love."

The orange glove waved to him with a movement like a caress. Then the window slid up, Manfred put the engine into gear, and the car was gone.

24

"Weird," Rick mused. He stuffed the money into his pocket and climbed back on his bike. It was in worse shape than he had initially suspected. The front rim was bent and the spokes were definitely damaged. He had to walk it the rest of the way. Fortunately, it wasn't much further.

The road levelled and Rick walked through the gates of Argo Manor. His eyes feasted on the scene, trying to absorb every detail – the flowers, the fountains, the incredible sight of the house itself. In a nearby garden, several gardening tools seemed to have been abruptly abandoned. In the courtyard ahead, Rick saw the reason why. The same black car that had run him off the road was parked there. And the red-haired woman, tall and impressive, was standing, nose to nose, with an old man with a white beard. She was gesturing wildly, pointing at the house, raising her voice.

The old man – it was Nestor, of course – remained impassive. He might as well have been listening to the buzzing of a fly. He shook his head slowly, raised his hands helplessly, and shrugged as if to say, "What can I do?"

Rick watched from a distance, unseen. When the argument was over, the woman's face was contorted with anger. She pointed a finger at Nestor and hissed, "This isn't over between us."

She slid into the car and slammed the door behind her. Manfred gunned the engine, made a sharp turn, and intentionally steered the car through a flower bed. It was a crude show of contempt.

Rick shook his head in disbelief and joined the old man as he knelt to inspect the ruined flowers. "Are you all right?" he asked.

Nestor looked up at Rick, surprised. Then his gaze returned to his ruined garden, a deep rut of tyre tracks running through it. The old man looked at the sun, closed his eyes, and sighed. He gave Rick a weary smile. "Her name is Oblivia Newton," Nestor explained. "She is not used to the word 'No'." He paused. "And you must be the boy from town."

"Rick Banner," the boy said, extending his hand.

"Jason and Julia have been expecting you," Nestor said, shaking Rick's hand. "They're inside."

Rick cast a long look at the imposing front door of Argo Manor and hesitated.

"What's wrong? Having second thoughts?" Nestor asked. "You've come a long way to stand outside and gape like a tourist. Go on, see for yourself," he urged.

He limped off in the direction of his gardening tools.

"Um, yeah," Rick called after him. "Right. Thanks. I'll just . . . go . . . inside."

He took a big breath. A part of him couldn't believe he was finally about to enter mysterious Argo Manor. He had the sudden urge to tell the old man that he, too, had a good reason to dislike Oblivia Newton. She had run him off the road! Nearly killed him! But when he turned, the old man had disappeared.

"Pretty fast for an old guy with a dodgy leg," Rick muttered.

– Chapter 4 –
HAUNTED

The first room Rick entered was open and spacious. It was like a porch, library, and sitting room all in one. Three large picture windows flooded the room with light, providing a view of the cliff edge and beyond. Shelves along the walls were filled with stacks of hardback books and magazines. Newspapers rested on a crystal-topped table. In the centre of the room was a life-sized statue of a woman mending a fishing net that hung in folds down from her hands. The fisherwoman gazed out at a fixed point in the sea, a dreamy look on her face. Rick stared at it. Suddenly, she seemed familiar to him.

"Nice room, isn't it?" asked Jason, appearing suddenly in the doorway.

Rick grinned. "Very," he replied.

"Well, I'm glad you're here," Jason said warmly. "Maybe you can help us find our way around – we still feel a bit lost in all these rooms."

They circled around the statue.

"Apparently the previous owner insisted that the statue should never be moved from this spot," Jason told Rick.

"Really? That's weird," Rick commented.

Jason shrugged. "I guess that was part of the deal, I don't exactly know." He added, "They say that he was a little crazy."

Rick nodded. "That's what they say."

Jason continued, "But I don't see how he can have any say over what we do, now that he's dead. I mean, *if* he's really dead..."

Rick frowned. "What does that mean, if he's really dead?"

"It means my brother has plenty of crazy ideas," Julia's voice broke in. She gave Rick a wry smile.

Though Jason and Julia were twins, their personalities were as different as the sun and the moon. Apart from the fact that one was a boy and the other a girl, Jason and Julia had the same light-coloured hair, the same eyes, the same dimpled cheeks. But Julia was slightly taller and more athletic than Jason, as if she were in more of a hurry to grow up. And their minds – the way they thought about things – made them almost total opposites.

Julia plopped down into one of the armchairs near the statue of the fisherwoman. "I've been listening to Jason tell wild stories since we first arrived from the city," she told Rick. "Dad says he has an 'over-active imagination'. Maybe one day he'll write all his stories down and become famous."

Jason blushed, embarrassed.

Rick sensed Jason's discomfort. "I promise to read all your stories after you become famous," he said with a smile. "But until then, do you think we could go exploring?"

Julia looked at Rick sharply. "You aren't another explorer-type, are you?" she asked him.

"In a place like this? Of course! Who wouldn't be? I'd want to check out every room, every dark cupboard, find secret stairways and hidden trap-doors. . ."

Jason's face lit up. "Can I tell you something?" he interrupted. "I think this house is. . ."

"Oh, no! Please don't start that again!" Julia protested.

Rick looked from Julia to Jason. "Go on," he said. "What were you going to say?"

"I think it's haunted," Jason finished.

Julia squirmed in her armchair. "That's right, folks," she said, adopting a voice like a radio DJ's. "You're listening to W-A-C-K-O, wacko on your radio dial! And the hits just keep on coming," she joked.

Rick looked back and forth between the twins, realizing he was caught in the middle of an ongoing war between brother and sister. He considered how to answer without offending one or the other. He didn't want to disappoint Jason, but he didn't want to look foolish in front of Julia, either.

The solution? Answer with another question:

"Why do you think there's a ghost?" he asked Jason.

"I've heard footsteps upstairs when nobody is here but me," Jason explained. His eyes were wide and earnest. "But mostly, it's a feeling. Just this weird sense I have about this house. Like there's a presence watching us."

"Oh, please," Julia groaned. "What will it be tonight? Chains in the hallway, screaming in the attic, or just furious flushing from the toilet?"

"Why don't you ever believe me, Julia?" Jason complained. "I'm telling you, I heard footsteps on the first floor. I was downstairs. You were asleep. Everybody else was outside. . ."

"You have to know one thing, Rick," Julia interrupted. "Jason reads about this stuff all the time. Of course he hears ghosts. It's all he ever *thinks* about – vampires, werewolves, zombies, and ghosts!"

Rick studied Jason. If Julia's remarks upset him, you couldn't tell by his face. In fact, Jason wore a slight smirk, as if he enjoyed Julia's comments. That's when it hit Rick. It was like a dance the twins had been rehearsing for years. They knew every step, every beat. They had had this argument hundreds of times. Because . . . *they liked it*!

"Jason thinks that Argo Manor is the home of a

famous ghost," Julia said, standing up and stretching. "Take a guess who it is."

Rick felt a little shiver ripple through him. "Ulysses Moore," he whispered.

Jason nodded. "Because he left something unresolved behind," he said.

Rick looked at Julia. "What can I say?" she said with a shrug. "His lift doesn't run to the top. He's got bats in his belfry. He's my twin – and I love him – but he's completely nuts." And with that, she swooped over and hugged Jason from behind.

Rick was still thinking about the ghost of Ulysses Moore. "Something unresolved," he murmured. "OK, let's say that makes sense. I wonder what it could be?"

Julia's eyes rolled. She plopped back down in her chair.

"I haven't worked that out yet," Jason answered Rick. "I need to learn more. I've been in Kilmore Cove for less than two weeks. I don't know this house very well yet."

"No wonder," Rick replied. "It's enormous."

Jason's eyes shone. He had an idea. "Hey, let's explore it room by room," he suggested. "We can even make a map."

"Oh, what fun," muttered Julia. "Hold on while I do the dance of joy."

Rick paid her no attention. "I'd love to make a map of this house," he blurted out. "That would be fantastic! To be honest, I've explored this house practically every day—from the outside, that is. For me, it would be the greatest. Man, just being here, with this statue and the books and you guys. All my life this place has felt like a magnet, drawing me here. Yeah, if you guys are up for it, I'm all for exploring every inch of this place."

Jason leaped up. "I'll get some paper and a pen. Back in a second."

He raced out of the room, leaving Rick and Julia alone for the first time.

Julia looked out at the sea, washed with white-capped waves. "You never said whether or not you believe in ghosts," she said. Her gaze fell on Rick's eyes. Her expression became suddenly intense and serious. "My brother and I may be different, but don't let that fool you. He's my best friend in the whole world. Are you playing around with him, or do you really believe in this stuff?"

Rick leaned against the statue of the fisherwoman, which felt solid and surprisingly warm.

"My father used to say that ghosts exist," Rick told Julia. "He said that each of us has his own personal ghost. Everyone is haunted by something."

Julia nodded. "So who's your ghost?"

"He is," Rick answered, his face turning hard. "My father. He died two years ago. And every day, he's with me."

They sat in silence, looking at the sea until Jason returned.

- Chapter 5 -
THE MAP

The children started out by exploring the first floor, working methodically room by room, and then went down to the ground floor. They set up their base in the stone room, the oldest room in the house, and began to draw a map of Argo Manor.

Rick naturally fell into the role of the leader. No one voted on it. That was simply the way it was. He was the one who took the lead, and Julia and Jason instantly respected his decisions. Whatever it is that makes a leader – bravery or strength or force of personality – Rick seemed to have it.

Now he was bent studiously over the hand-drawn map. "There are three chimneys," he noted. "One in the kitchen, one here, and the other outside. Four bathrooms. Two large dining rooms. Five bedrooms. One library, a smaller library, and. . ." Rick squinted. "What have you written here, Julia?"

"Private study," Julia answered. "That's the room with that massive, ancient desk. The one next to the library with the painted ceiling."

"And one private study," Rick concluded. "Is this staircase the one with all the paintings?" he asked, pointing to the map.

"No. That's the one that leads down to the cellar," Jason answered.

Rick nodded. The cellar. So far, they hadn't given

that a good look. It was an immense space – dank and dark and dusty – and it was packed with old furniture and boxes that were stacked to the ceiling in such a way that the only free space left was a narrow passageway.

"The cellar gives me the creeps," Julia said.

No one disagreed.

"If I were a ghost, that's the last place I'd stay," she continued.

Jason raised his eyebrows in surprise. "I thought you didn't believe in ghosts."

"Hey, I'm just playing along," Julia replied. "It's not like there's anything else to do around here in Dullsville."

"Sure, Julia," Jason commented knowingly. "You're just playing along." He turned back to the map and gazed at it thoughtfully, chewing on the end of his pen. "All that's left is the room with the tower at the top of the stairs," he pointed out. "Then we're finished with all the main rooms."

"The lighthouse room," murmured Rick.

"Why do you call it that?" Jason asked.

"Every night, Ulysses Moore seemed to be up there," Rick answered. "The light in that room was always on through the night, as if old Ulysses wanted to compete with the other lighthouse, the real one, on the other side of the bay."

They remained in silence for a few moments, imagining the light of the tower atop the cliff shining out, a beacon in the darkness calling distant travellers home.

"Do you know anything about him, Rick?" Julia asked. "Ulysses Moore, I mean."

"He was mysterious," Rick answered with a shrug. "I don't think anybody knows much about him. He was a recluse. Just a rich eccentric who seemed to live in his own world."

The twins looked at each other, intrigued.

"He was really . . . *original*, you see," Rick continued. "Ulysses kept to himself. He never went into town. Not once."

"In forty years?"

"In forty years," Rick confirmed.

"How could that be possible?" Julia asked incredulously.

Rick just shook his head. "The story is that Ulysses was married to a beautiful, dark-haired woman. My mother knew her. She would occasionally come down into town to run errands, to buy some fish, pick up the post. Just normal stuff that people do. But Ulysses? He was never seen there."

Rick paused. "And then she died."

Julia found herself becoming more and more fascinated. Jason listened calmly, as if absorbing every word through the pores of his skin.

"How did she die?" Julia asked.

"Again," Rick replied, "that's another mystery. They say that Ulysses never called a doctor, never brought her to the hospital. One day, she was dead. That's all anybody knows."

"Wow," Julia said.

"After she died," Rick added, "Ulysses sent the caretaker on the errands."

"Nestor?"

"You got it," Rick confirmed. "As far as I know, Nestor began working here when the wife was still alive, not long before she died. In a way, I guess Nestor replaced her. He ran all of old man Moore's errands."

"That is soooo weird," Julia said. "The guy never left the house. He trades in a bewitching wife for a grumpy old man? I don't get it."

"There's more," Rick said. "Long ago, before I was born, they say he had a big ship anchored in the inlet at the bottom of the cliff."

"Right!" Jason blurted out. "I saw steps going down! We should definitely check that out."

"Forget the boat, Popeye," Julia interrupted. "I

still want to know why he never went into town. Was he hiding something? Or was he just some kind of freak?"

Rick tilted his head thoughtfully. "With Ulysses Moore, it's impossible to know the real truth. There are stories and legends, rumours and lies. Nobody knows exactly what to believe. . . "

"Except for Nestor," Jason said. "Nestor must know the truth."

Rick nodded. Julia felt an unexpected shiver run down her spine.

"One story is that he had a horrible scar that went all the way across his face," Rick told the twins. "He was ashamed of it. That's why he never showed his face in town."

"But it's just a story," Jason said. "We don't know for sure."

"The painting!" Julia blurted out. "The portraits along the stairs!"

She grabbed Jason's arm so suddenly, he nearly swallowed the pen lid. He gagged and coughed, and the pen fell to the floor, rolling under the large wardrobe.

"Sorry about that," said Julia. "But there's no time to choke and die right now. We have work to do. Follow me!"

Julia swept out of the room. She called over her

shoulder, "Let's go and see the hideous face of Ulysses Moore!"

Rick and Jason looked at each other and shrugged, then fell into step behind her.

They followed the long line of portraits up the stairs. One by one, they read the names and dates. But the portraits suddenly ended in the mid twentieth century.

"Oh my God," Julia whispered when they reached the top of the stairs. "It's not here."

Rick was disappointed. "Bummer. It looks like they never got around to doing a painting."

"No," Jason said. "They did a painting all right. It used to hang right here." He pointed to a blank space on the wall.

Julia frowned. "How do you know?"

"Look closely," Jason said. "This area has been repainted. The colour is just a little bit off."

"Maybe," Rick said. "No, wait, yes. I can see it now. You're right. There used to be something here, and the wall has been repainted."

"Why repaint it?" Julia asked.

"There would have been an outline on the wall," Rick explained. "The wall behind the painting would have been protected from dust and dirt."

"It would have been a clue," Jason said. "A clue that someone went to a lot of effort to get rid of."

A thousand questions ran through their minds. Why? Who? When? They all talked excitedly. Jason suddenly raised a hand to silence Julia and Rick. He cocked his head, listening. "Did you hear that?" he whispered.

"Hear what?" Julia replied.

"I did," Rick answered. His eyes climbed the stairs until they landed on a door. "It came from up there."

"Hello? Guys!" Julia snapped. "Let's not get all freaky, OK? You're probably just. . ."

Then she heard it, too.

A muffled sound, a thump.

". . .hearing things," Julia said doubtfully.

The three friends turned slowly towards the mirrored door at the top of the steps. The door that led to the tower room. The lighthouse room.

The noise was coming from there.

They stood in silence, hearts thundering, listening for what felt like an eternity. But the sound didn't come again. And so, grouped tightly together, they slowly approached the door. The mirror reflected their image: three young children, serious, excited, frightened.

Jason reached out his hand, put it on the doorknob, paused for a moment, then turned it. The door opened slightly, just enough so he could peek inside. He hoped to surprise whoever – or whatever – was inside.

"What can you see?" Rick whispered from over Jason's shoulder.

In answer, Jason opened the door wider to reveal the entire room. There was a large table positioned at an angle between two windows looking out over the sea, a collection of model ships and magazines stacked up on the ground. Through the windows, the children had a stunning view of the cliff, Kilmore Cove, and the grounds below.

"Nothing's here," whispered Jason, looking around. "No ghosts."

"How could that be?" Julia asked. "What made the noise?"

Almost in answer, there came the sound of footsteps.

Ta-thump, ta-thump.

Only it wasn't footsteps. One of the windows was slightly ajar, and every so often it banged against its frame, making the rhythmic noise that first Jason and then the others had mistaken for footsteps.

"Some ghost," Julia sighed. "It was just the wind."

But instead of relief, the three ghost-hunters felt a pang of disappointment. It was like air seeping out of a balloon.

"Still, what a great view," said Julia, staring out of the window.

Rick scanned the grounds of Argo Manor. He saw the gate, the gravel-covered courtyard, and the small wooden house where Nestor lived – the caretaker's quarters.

Meanwhile, Jason sat down at the table, taking a few moments to imagine that he was master of the house. He wanted to know how it must have felt for Ulysses Moore, working here late in the evening, night after night.

Jason delicately ran his finger along one of the many model ships which, arranged on top of a chest, formed a miniature fleet painstakingly crafted by hand.

I can feel you, Ulysses, Jason thought to himself. *I understand what you must have felt to sit here, alone with your thoughts, far from the world.*

He turned to the others and announced, "He must have sat right here at this table, passing away the hours by building these little ships."

A wave crashed against the rocks below, raising up an explosion of froth and foam.

"Let's go for a swim!" Julia said.

As usual, Julia did not wait for a reply. Her mind was made up. She left the bewildered boys behind as she ran to find her swimming costume.

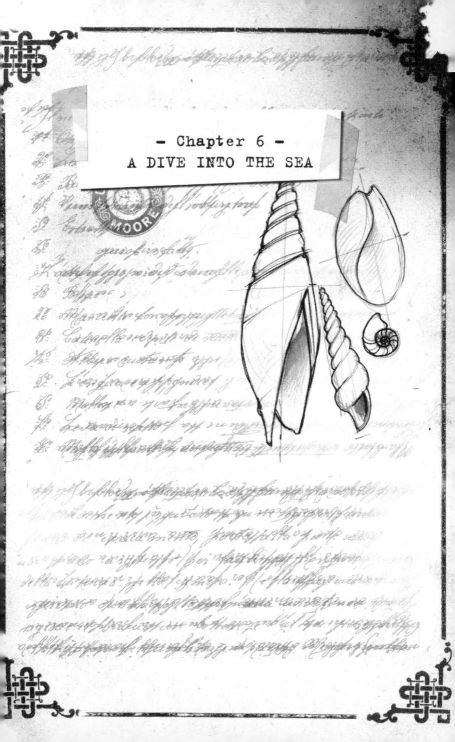

- Chapter 6 -
A DIVE INTO THE SEA

Outside, they ran into Nestor. The old caretaker eyed them suspiciously. Rick, Jason, and Julia were wearing their swimming things and carrying towels.

Nestor gave them a disapproving stare. "And where exactly do you think you're going?"

They stood frozen in place, not sure how to answer.

Nestor couldn't keep a straight face. He broke into a smile, threw his head back and laughed, then turned back to his gardening.

Julia was irritated. "That's it?" she said to Nestor. "You look at us and laugh. That's how you take care of us?"

"What would you like me to tell you?" Nestor asked. The old man picked up a small begonia and turned it carefully in his fingers as though it were a precious stone. "What should I say? Be careful on the steps! Don't run. Don't trip. Don't drown. Don't get kidnapped. Don't, don't, don't, don't."

Nestor smiled happily. His eyes twinkled. "I say, *do. Do* and have fun doing it!"

"I've never met anyone like him before," Julia muttered, moving cautiously along the stone steps that led down to the seaside. There was something about Nestor that made her slightly uncomfortable.

The cliffside steps looked treacherous. Supposedly they were solidly built. But one slip and, well, it was a long way down.

The path consisted of flights of steps carved directly into the rock. These alternated with walkways of wood and metal, under which one could see the froth of the sea swirling around the rocks. At the top of the cliff Julia felt almost dizzy from the height, and the sea below seemed unreal to her. But now it came into focus with each step. It grew louder – and more dangerous – as the waves pounded an outcropping of rock. Julia was no longer sure that swimming was such a great idea.

The children made their way slowly, holding on to guide ropes with both hands. The wind whipped through their hair, bringing with it the smell of seaweed and wet sand. As they climbed down further, the steps became damper and more slippery from the sea spray.

"I like the old guy," Rick said of Nestor.

"I don't know," Julia said. "There's something about him I don't trust."

Jason half-listened, gazing dreamily at the sea. He barely watched where he was going. Already he was in love – with Kilmore Cove, with Argo Manor, with his new life in this place. Unlike his sister, Jason was glad to be away from the city, the noise, and the confusion. It was too much for him. But here at Argo Manor, in this world, he felt at home.

Rick was the last one down. He paused to look up along the ridges of the cliff. It was as if he was trying to see something that he couldn't quite explain. The truth was, Rick had the uneasy feeling that they were being watched. Once he even seemed to catch a glimpse of reflected light. And that reflection was enough for him to imagine that Nestor was keeping watch on them through a pair of binoculars. Maybe he was more concerned about their safety than he had let on. Or maybe he watched them for other, unknown reasons.

At last, the three reached an isolated cove – a stretch of beach nestled between two outcrops of rock. It was sheltered from the wind and from curious eyes. Argo Manor towered high over them, bathed in sunlight. The seagulls wheeled around their nests built into the crevices in the rocks, their throaty cries ringing out.

"Beautiful," Julia said, admiring their graceful flight.

"Rats with wings," Rick said scornfully. "They're scavengers, and they'll eat anything."

Julia frowned. "That's what people in London say about the pigeons, but I don't care. I like them."

In this part of the cove, the water was calm, protected from the waves by the rocks. Julia dropped her towel on the sand and rushed into the sea. The water was freezing but refreshing.

She disappeared under the water and, like a seal, came back up to the surface ten metres further out. She swam with powerful strokes, her body lithe and strong.

"Come on!" she shouted, pushing her hair back. "It's fantastic!"

And she was right. The sandy floor of the inlet stretched out into the sea, remaining shallow for several metres. Along the row of rocks, the sea spray created tiny rainbows that danced in the sunlight. The sound of the waves was almost magical. Enchanting. Like a siren's call, hypnotic and alluring.

Rick dived in and swam with effortless confidence. Julia couldn't help but admire his strength and grace in the water.

Jason stayed on the shore, his arms crossed, water lapping at his feet.

"Come on in, Jason," Julia urged. She confided to Rick, "He's always been like this. He's more of a watcher. And he likes being alone."

Rick nodded. The droplets of water in Julia's hair were like little pearls. He liked being with her, floating in the sea together. It was turning out to be an awesome day.

From the top of the cliff, Nestor smiled. He could hear the children's distant laughter, and he knew that the three of them had reached the beach safe and sound. It was good to hear young voices at the house. Maybe, just maybe, he was right. There was something special about those two and their friend. Maybe the old magic would come back.

He returned to the flowers, thrusting his hands into the earth. He decided not to think about it. Or worry. Or fear. Whatever would come, would come. And come what may, he would be ready.

But still Nestor thought of Jason, Julia and Rick. It would be good to wake up in the morning and imagine a new day. Their questions, their curiosity. They were alive. They were open to new things, new adventures. And if they were really special, as gifted as he hoped they were . . . who knew?

For now, there was only the sound of their laughter carried by the wind. Laughter. That was something that had not been heard at Argo Manor for a long, long time.

"Nothing better," the old man murmured. "Nothing better."

He pressed his fingers down into the fresh earth, looking for the best spot for the small roots of his tender young flowers.

Jason, Julia and Rick were lying stomach-down on their towels, lining up some of the treasures they'd fished out of the sand: an assortment of coloured rocks and shells, and a piece of wood with an iron bolt attached to it. To get the wood, Rick had swum out all the way to the very edge of the rocks, where the sea got deeper and the current started to pull at him, like a hand grabbing at his legs. Rick felt it was wiser not to go further out, and Julia happily agreed with him. There was no sense risking their lives when they had everything they needed right here.

Julia flipped on to her back to sunbathe while Rick and Jason explored the cove. They discovered a second stretch of beach, where there were traces of a small wooden jetty. A number of mooring lines hung from it. The walkways and boards had almost completely rotted away, but the remnants stood as evidence that old Ulysses had once, in fact, kept a boat here.

Jason was daydreaming about the old man's adventures as he and Rick went back to tell the news to Julia, who had become thoroughly bored with sunbathing. That was typical of Julia. She could sit still for fifteen minutes, tops. She sat up and hugged her knees as Jason told her about what he and Rick had found. His telling made their adventure on the rocks take on mystical proportions.

While Jason spoke, Rick felt a raindrop on his face. He looked up. A dark cloud crossed overhead. "Rain," he announced.

Jason looked at the long series of steps that wound their way up towards home. A long, hard climb awaited them. "Should we start going back up?" he asked.

"We'd better," Rick decided. "It may be only a shower, but you never know. We should be careful."

Julia agreed. Anything was better than sitting around in the rain.

The rain came harder now. The steps were more slippery than ever. Jason struggled to keep up with his athletic sister and friend. In a burst of energy, he pushed them aside and sprinted up the stairs in twos and threes. He couldn't last at that pace, but at least he'd get a head start.

"See you up at the top, suckers!" he shouted.

Julia turned to Rick. "Come on, let's race," she urged.

But Rick surprised her. His face was calm, content. "Let him go," Rick said. "He gets to win while we take it nice and slow. Together."

Suddenly, Jason screamed. Rick and Julia looked up just in time to see him tumbling, falling, clawing for his life along the cliff.

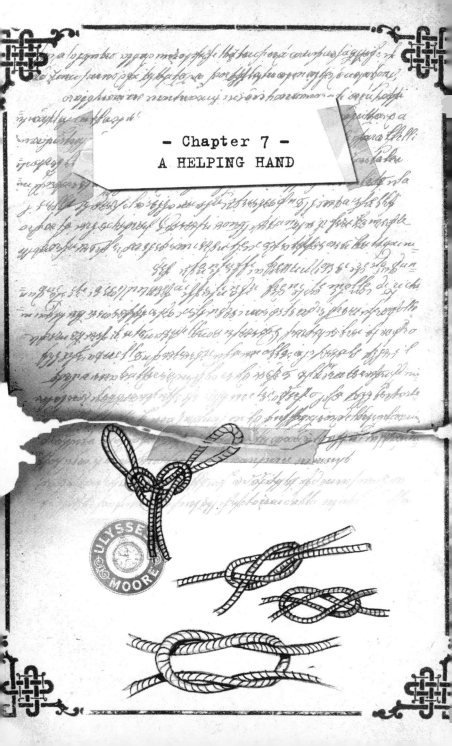

- Chapter 7 -
A HELPING HAND

Jason's first thought – the one he immediately had when his left foot slipped, when he lost his balance – was this: *Stupid me.*

He slid down against the granite face of the cliff. It felt like someone was rubbing a cheese grater against his chest. His hands pawed against the rock and managed to cling to a crevice. That's how Jason thought of it, too: his hands took over while he – sort of – *watched*. It was all animal instinct and reaction. His hands found the rock. His body saved itself.

Strangely, Jason wasn't panicked. Not in the least. Instead, he felt an eerie calm. A kind of slow-motion replay that you see in football matches, as if he were watching himself from a great distance. Falling, falling.

His fingers held on to an edge of rock. They held tight.

Jason was no longer falling.

He was dangling.

Hanging on to a crevice in the rock with both hands.

And still, for some reason, he was not afraid.

Go figure.

Of course, Julia and Rick were scared out of their minds.

"Hold on!" Rick shouted. "We'll help you."

Julia's mind swirled with images and fractured thoughts. But no words came. She ran with Rick up the stairs to the exact point where Jason had fallen. He was just a few metres below them, but out of reach.

Rick's eyes darted about as he quickly assessed the scene. He searched for something, anything, that might be of use. A stick? A loose piece of board? The towels? Yes, the towels – maybe make them into some kind of rope. He looked down at Jason. Could he hold on long enough? Jason was not strong; there wasn't much time.

Then he saw it. To Jason's right, not far at all, there was a small ledge. Just a few centimetres down and over.

Julia was growing increasingly frantic. Her eyes looked wild, her damp hair tangled in front of her face. She was shaking.

"Stay calm," Rick told her. He grabbed Julia by the shoulders. "Do you hear me? If you want to save Jason, you've got to stay calm and do exactly as I say."

Julia's wild eyes slowly gained focus. She looked at Rick and blinked, nodding. "Right, right," she said. "Stay calm."

Meanwhile, Jason's arm muscles were beginning to burn. His fingers deadened. And his grip began to slip. Rick glanced down, worried.

"Here." He shoved the two towels into Julia's hands. "Tear them in strips, like this." Rick pulled the towel, tearing it lengthwise. "Then tie the ends together. Do you see? We'll make a rope."

"Um, guys?" Jason said. "Sorry to bother you, but I'm slipping."

Julia began tearing at the towel.

Rick turned to Jason. He knelt down, trying to get as close as possible. "Listen to me, Jason. There's a small ledge to your right. Can you see it?"

Jason shook his head.

"Look down to your right," Rick instructed. "You can do this, Jason. Can you see that ledge?"

Jason turned his head, glancing downward. He nodded sharply. He saw it.

"You are going to have to climb along the rock wall," Rick said, "like a spider. First one hand, then a foot, then the other hand, then the other foot. Do you understand?"

"Like a spider," Jason said.

There he was, hanging from a crevice in the rock twenty metres from the ground, and he felt clear-headed and in control. It was bizarre. It was as if the hand of fate had reached out to him, had plucked him out to do this one thing, and there was no way that he could fail.

He knew exactly what to do.

Not that it would be easy.

Jason felt blindly along the rock wall, his fingers seeking something to hold on to. His legs trembled from the strain. And he fought with everything he had, he endured every ache, and at last his feet found a secure ledge carved into the cliff. His arms loosened. If balanced correctly, he could almost stand. Finally reassured, Jason managed to look up.

And smile.

"I'm all right," he said.

Rick and Julia exchanged relieved glances. Rick was checking the knots, pulling on the ends of the rope-towel. "Good work," he told Julia.

Rick tied one end to a stair railing above Jason. The other end dangled down within Jason's reach. "Grab hold," Rick told him. "We'll pull you up."

By now Jason was filled with confidence. He was a spider. He could do whatever was necessary. He could climb to safety even without a rope – Jason felt it in his bones. All he had to do was slowly, carefully feel along the rock and. . .

What was that?

His hand found . . . a hole? No, an opening. Was it a nest of some kind? The home of a cliff-dwelling bird?

Jason looked at it more closely. The opening was a perfect rectangle. Carved by a man-made tool. And it was deep, like the sleeve of a coat.

"Wait a second," Jason called up. "There's something here!"

Jason reached inside the opening and felt something soft against his hand. It was a fabric of some kind. Then, for a reason he could not explain, not then, or ever, Jason sensed there was a cave behind the cliff. He didn't *think* it *might* be there. He *knew* it was there.

Jason withdrew his hand and realized that he was holding something small and brick-shaped. It was wrapped in cloth.

"Jason, grab on to the rope," Rick cried.

"Please, Jason!" Julia pleaded.

Jason snapped out of his thoughts. He stuffed the object into his swimming trunks, grabbed the rope with both hands, and began to climb with his legs.

When Rick and Julia had helped pull him up to safety, all the strength seemed to drain from Jason's body. He was exhausted.

Julia threw her arms around him. "Are you OK?" she asked her twin in a hushed voice.

He was. But he couldn't answer. He just smiled. He was safe at last.

The three friends stood in a tight clump, breathing hard. Finally, Jason pulled out the object he'd discovered. "Look at what I found," he said.

"Never mind that," Julia said crossly. "You're scratched all over, bleeding. We need to get back to the house. Now."

Jason blinked. Scratches? Bleeding? He looked at his chest, his arms and legs. His skin was rubbed raw in places, scratched, bruised, and bloodied. He suddenly felt light-headed. He looked down to where he had climbed from.

"How did I do that?" he wondered aloud. "What happened?"

"Not now," Rick said, pulling Jason to his feet. "Don't talk. Here, hold on to me. One at a time, up these steps. Nice and slow."

Together the three friends made their way up the cliff face. Jason still gripped the object he had found tightly.

- Chapter 8 -
THE CODE

"Ouch! That stings," Jason complained.

"Good, I'm glad," Julia replied, applying more antiseptic to her brother's wounds. "It serves you right for almost getting yourself killed." She paused before adding, "It would have ruined my entire weekend."

"You're enjoying this," Jason muttered.

Julia smiled, then dabbed him with more antiseptic. "Yes, I think I am."

Rick just shook his head. Watching the two of them made him wish he had a brother or sister.

Julia stepped back to take a look at her patient. Jason sat at the kitchen table, shirtless. He looked like a mess from the fall, but none of the scrapes were deep.

Jason turned to Rick. "Have you figured out what that is yet?"

On the table between them was the mysterious object Jason had found hidden inside the cliff. Rick slowly pulled at the cloth that was wrapped around the box. "It's like they are bandages, or I should say *were* bandages," Rick commented. He slowly unravelled the cloth.

"It's a wooden box," Jason whispered.

"Cool," Rick said. He pressed on the upper panel of the box and it slid sideways. "It opens up!"

Jason and Julia leaned forward. "What is that stuff?" Jason asked.

It was a mystery all right. Inside the box there were dozens of little brown balls that seemed to be made of clay. How odd . . . and how disappointing.

Julia deadpanned, "Oh joy, we've found an old box of chocolate-covered cherries. I'll alert the media."

Rick poked his finger inside the box. Underneath the balls was a small tube of parchment tied with string. It looked ancient.

"Careful," murmured Jason as Rick lifted it from the box.

Rick very slowly untied the parchment. He carefully unrolled the yellowed paper on to the table. On it were various drawings and symbols:

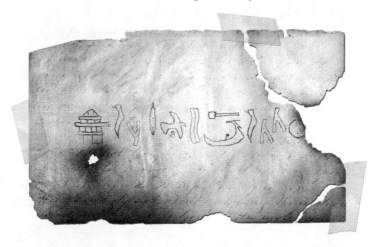

Julia looked from the paper to the puzzled faces of her two friends. "Can anybody here read Egyptian?"

Nestor was working in the greenhouse, where he had taken refuge from the brief afternoon rain. The old man had always enjoyed it there, especially during a shower, when the water drummed against the sloping windows of the greenhouse. Now the sun shone through the clouds, glistening on the drops of rain that still clung to the grass and flowers.

He was not worried about Julia, Jason, and Rick. *Wet from the ocean, wet from the rain,* he thought. *In the end, there's no difference.*

But now Nestor saw them gathered outside the greenhouse, anxiously waiting for him to finish his work. He turned his back to them for several minutes, completed the task at hand, then cleaned up and joined them outside.

"What do you want?" asked Nestor gruffly. "I've got work to do."

Julia elbowed her brother. "Ow," he complained. She had forgotten about his scrapes. Jason looked to the sky, the ground, anywhere but into the old man's iron gaze. Then finally he spoke. "I was wondering, I mean, we were wondering – since you've lived here for a while and everything – Julia thought we should ask, and, you see, the thing is. . ."

Nestor tapped his foot impatiently. He pretended to check the time on an imaginary watch. "Is this going to take all afternoon?"

Jason thrust the parchment into Nestor's hands. "We found this," he hurriedly explained. "And we were kind of thinking that maybe you might know how to read it."

Nestor observed the three children closely. Rick, clear-eyed and pragmatic; Jason, nervous, dreamy, but full of hope and determination; and Julia, sharp-witted and tough.

Nestor rolled open the parchment. "How did you get this?" he asked. His tone was deadly serious.

They led Nestor to the edge of the cliff, where the steps began their descent. Jason explained how he had slipped, and pointed to where he found the box. He glossed over the details of the fall, leaving out how close he'd been to tumbling to his death. The last thing he needed was for his overprotective mother to find out about that. She'd never let him out of the house again.

Nestor listened to Jason's tale with rapt attention. When Jason finished his story, the caretaker stood quietly musing. He seemed to be listening to the waves as they crashed against the rocks. But to Rick it felt as if the old man was trying to make up his mind about something.

Finally, Nestor returned the parchment to Jason. He shook his head. "I don't know what it means," he concluded. "No idea at all."

"But it's writing of some kind, don't you think?" Jason countered. "Like hieroglyphics, maybe."

Nestor scowled. "I've seen hieroglyphic writing," he replied. "It does not look like these . . . silly doodles."

"Doodles!" echoed Jason in disbelief. "It looks like more than just doodles to me."

Rick chimed in. "Nestor is right, Jason. It can't be hieroglyphic writing. That's Egyptian. This paper is parchment, and the ancient Egyptians wrote on papyrus. Plus, I kind of doubt an Egyptian came all the way to this part of England just to hide a secret message."

"Why not?" Jason asked.

"Because they weren't good sailors," Rick responded. "The Egyptians had boats made of woven reeds, which were good for floating along the Nile. But they could never have endured a rough passage across an open sea."

Nestor gave Rick an appreciative nod. He was clever, that one. And like so many boys who grew up in Kilmore Cove, Rick obviously had a fascination with the sea. *This one is promising,* thought the old man. *There is hope for this boy.*

"Maybe it's just a practical joke," Julia offered. "A prank or something."

"That's ridiculous, Julia," Jason said. "This box must be important. Why else would somebody hide it inside a cliff? It has to mean something."

Julia crossed her arms. "It doesn't *have* to mean anything."

"Maybe it's some sort of map or secret message," Jason said. "Maybe an old pirate made Kilmore Cove his base and hid his treasure somewhere around here."

Julia rolled her eyes. "Great, just great. First a ghost, now a pirate. What's next, Jason? A little green man from Mars?"

"Perhaps. . ." the caretaker began, then shook his head. "No, no. It can't be."

"Perhaps what?" Jason said.

"Listen." Nestor turned to Jason. "Forget all this talk of treasure and secret messages. This is all a fantasy."

"Perhaps what?" Jason repeated once more.

He was insistent. "What were you going to say?"

Nestor sighed, surrendering to the boy's determination. "Ulysses Moore was a student of ancient languages," the old man told them. "He had many books about secret writings, codes, and lost languages. I myself don't understand any of it. But if you wish, I'm sure you could look in Mr Moore's library. Maybe with the help of those books, you can find out the meaning of the message."

Jason's eyes widened. He was surprised by Nestor's sudden, unexpected help. "Really? Um, thanks. Thanks a lot."

"Let's go and find the books," Rick said.

"Some mystery," Julia muttered. "It sounds like homework to me." But she followed her brother and Rick as they ran towards the house.

- Chapter 9 -
THE LIBRARY

The library was on the first floor. It was an impressive room, like a shrine to human knowledge. Its ceiling was painted with red and blue medallions. Natural light flooded in from two large windows that overlooked the courtyard gardens. Bookshelves filled every wall from floor to ceiling. There was a sofa covered with what appeared to be buffalo skin, a gorgeous grand piano, and several overstuffed armchairs. Various sections of the bookshelves were labelled with copper plaques that indicated the books' topics: history, medicine, geography, and so on.

The three immediately set out to find the books Nestor had described.

"It must be this section here," Julia decided at one point.

"What does it say?" called Rick from across the room.

"Palaeography."

"Palaeo . . . what?" Rick asked.

"If I remember correctly," Julia explained, "in Greek *palaeo* means 'ancient'. Like Palaeolithic man. And *grafia* or *graphy* means 'writing'."

Rick looked at her, impressed. "You're full of surprises," he said.

Julia shrugged. "I try."

Rick was the tallest among them, so he got up on

tiptoe and grabbed a thick book entitled *Dictionary of Forgotten Languages*. "This looks promising," he said. He quickly leafed through the pages. There were dozens of images and symbols that reconstructed ancient forms of writing: the Phoenician alphabet, an Indian alphabet, Egyptian hieroglyphs, the mysterious Etruscan language, the Greek alphabet, the unknown Rongorongo script from Easter Island, and many others. Each page contained symbols, drawings, secret codes and lost languages. It was like a treasury of everything that man had once known but had forgotten over the centuries.

As Rick turned the pages, Jason suddenly reached over and pointed. "Wait! Is that it?"

In the middle of the two pages was this drawing:

Above it were the words:

THE SYMBOLS OF THE PHAISTOS DISC

"It sure looks like them," Julia said.

Rick read aloud: "*These are the forty-five myste-rious figures depicted on the so-called Phaistos Disc. This object, a crudely rounded clay disc, was discov-ered on the island of Crete at the beginning of the twentieth century by archeologists Halbherr and Pernier, and has never been deciphered.*"

"Keep going," Julia whispered. She was getting swept up in the mystery in spite of herself.

"*On both of its sides, the disc bears an inscription arranged in a spiral, like a coiled snake. The letters that accompany the individual pictograms are part of an attempt to create a phonetic translation. This was done by palaeographer Elton Carter.*"

Beside each symbol, or figure, was its correspond-ing significance with a character from our alphabet.

"I get it," Jason said. "The walking man indicates the number one. The disc with the dots is the letter *a.*" He smoothed the parchment on to the table beside the dictionary.

Rick shook his head. "It won't be that easy," he stated. "It's not enough to know the meaning of the letters to decipher an ancient message. We also need to know the language it's written in. For all we know, this message could be written in ancient Greek."

"What makes you so sure it's ancient?" Julia questioned.

"Isn't it obvious?" Rick replied. He pointed to the text and read: "*The characters in the Phaistos Disc were used thousands of years before the birth of Christ.*"

The twins, however, refused to give up so easily. They began to write down the phonetic translation of each of the parchment's hieroglyphs.

Julia grinned at Rick. "Hey, there's no harm trying," she explained with a shrug. "Maybe it's a note saying we won the lottery."

"WHEN!" cried Jason, translating the first four characters.

Rick continued to shake his head doubtfully.

"THE!" cried Julia as they finished the second word.

"It does mean something!" Jason exclaimed.

The twins looked at each other, then at Rick, who stared back at them in awe. How could this be? Could the parchment contain a message in their own language, but written using an unknown alphabet? Why in the world would someone do that?

They were soon able to read the first complete line out loud:

"When the grotto's darkness seems defeat, these earth-lights. . ."

And then, at the worst possible moment, their pen ran out of ink.

"Oh, great!" complained Jason, shaking it furiously. "Find another pen!" he ordered Julia.

"Excuse me?" Julia said. "Who died and anointed you king?"

"Well, I don't know where to find a pen!" Jason snapped. "It could take hours to find one in this place!"

"Where's the one you were using to draw the map?" Rick intervened.

Jason thought for a moment, picturing it. He remembered that he had dropped it . . . and it had rolled . . . yes, beneath the big wardrobe. "It's downstairs," he said. "I'll be right back!"

Jason flew down the stairs and towards the stone room. Then he stopped suddenly. A shadow had passed before him, seemingly out of nowhere.

Jason was unable to speak. He stood trembling. *Something* was in the house.

From upstairs, muffled by the distance, came the

voices of his sister and Rick. Jason could hear their words:

"When the grotto's darkness seems defeat,
these earth-lights you . . . may . . . use!"

Gradually, Jason's sense of panic faded away. He looked around carefully, but didn't see anything suspicious. Was it just his imagination? A simple trick of the mind? Or was he somehow able to *feel* things – things that couldn't be seen?

He cautiously made his way to the stone room. Lying on the floor was the map they had abandoned when they'd gone to search for the portrait of Ulysses.

Jason crossed to the other side of the room, his senses alert. He knelt down beside the wardrobe and felt underneath it for the pen.

Unfortunately, it had rolled all the way back to the furthest edge, against the wall. As Jason strained to reach for the pen, he noticed something. The "wall" behind the wardrobe wasn't a wall at all. It was a different colour. He pressed against it with his fingers. It felt rough-hewn, wooden. No, it was not a wall at all.

Curious, Jason stood up and tried to move the enormous piece of furniture. It was very heavy, but he was able to shift it just far enough to get a better look at what lay behind it.

It was a door.

When Jason returned to the library, he handed the pen to Julia. Then he stood off to the side, troubled and thoughtful, while she and Rick finished translating the entire message.

Julia rewrote it on four lines, like a poem, and read it out loud with a triumphant voice:

"When the grotto's darkness seems defeat,
these earth-lights you may use
to shine a light upon the fleet
that takes you where you choose."

"What does that mean?" Rick wondered. "It was easier to understand before we translated it."

"Yeah, what he said," Julia agreed. "And what the heck is a grotto? Is that a cave or something?"

"Exactly," Rick answered. "It's like a cave or a cavern."

"There must be grottoes all over this area," Jason said thoughtfully.

"I've been digging around in caves my whole life," Rick said. "All the children around here do it."

Julia smirked. "That's because there's nothing better to do in Kilmore Cove. Go shopping? Nope. The cinema? Um, no. How about a museum and then a free concert in the park? Er, no. Instead, hey, I've got it. Let's all crawl around in dark, disgusting caves all day!"

Rick was slightly offended. "Sorry we're not the big city, Julia. You'll have to go somewhere else to find crime and pollution."

"Maybe I will," Julia shot back.

"Guys, guys," Jason interrupted. "Save the country mouse–city mouse argument for later. Let's get back to the grotto."

Rick and Julia laughed. Jason was right.

"OK. Well, there's a local legend," Rick began, "that the ancient druids used to meet in Kilmore Cove at the spring equinox. Supposedly their secret place was a 'grotto by the sea', but it collapsed or was destroyed during the Roman invasion two thousand years ago."

"Druids? Cool!" Julia exclaimed. Once again, she couldn't help but be drawn into the mystery. She listened closely as Rick tried to remember other local tales that mentioned grottoes or fleets, desperately trying to make sense of the word *earthlights*.

Jason, on the other hand, seemed strangely detached, remote. It seemed as if his mind was somewhere else.

"Jason," Julia finally asked. "Are you OK? You seem so out of it. Maybe you ought to lie down and rest." She nudged his shoulder.

Jason's eyes came back into focus. He shook his head, trying to snap out of it.

Julia stared hard at him. "You're freaking me out a bit, Jason," she said. "Here we are with a real mystery to solve, and you're staring off into space like a zombie from some B movie." She snapped her fingers. "Wake up! Did you hear what Rick was saying about the druids?"

Jason rubbed the side of his head. "I heard you," he muttered. "Druids."

Julia continued. "Rick says there was once a big grotto in Kilmore Cove, where the druids held their secret gatherings. . ."

"I know," Jason said softly. "I've seen it."

"What?"

"I know where it is," Jason told them.

"What do you mean, you know where it is?" Rick asked. "How could you possibly know that?"

Jason looked at Rick, then at Julia. He gave a slight shrug. "I don't know *how* I know," he replied, "but I swear to you, I'm sure of it. I just know."

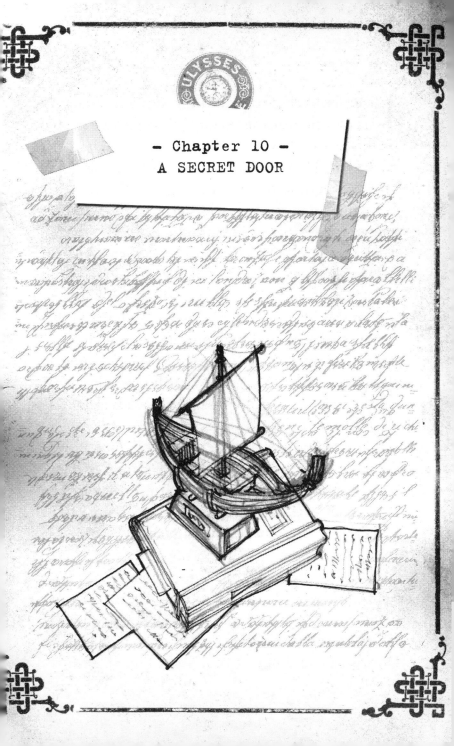

- Chapter 10 -
A SECRET DOOR

Jason led them down into the stone room again. Rick carried the dictionary, the box full of clay balls, the parchment with its translation and what seemed to be the only working pen in the entire house.

"I saw an open space, OK?" Jason insisted. "There was an empty space behind the rock."

Rick was doubtful. "You mean the cliff is hollow?"

Jason nodded.

"Let's say you're right," Rick responded. "That would explain how you managed to find the box. But –" he paused – "now we're talking about a much, much bigger hole than the one the box was in."

Julia read the box's message out loud again. She was, in her own words, "obsessing about it": "*When the grotto's darkness seems defeat . . . shine a light upon the fleet.*" She stopped and stared at them. "Wait a minute. It makes sense! It makes complete sense!" she cried. "The message talks about a fleet. And a fleet can only be found in the sea. Whoever wrote this message—"

"Ulysses Moore," Jason interrupted.

"What?"

"That message was written by Ulysses Moore," Jason stated. "Who else could it have been? It was written in English. He just used an alphabet from the Phaistos Disc to turn it into a code."

"*Okaaay*, sure. But why?" Julia asked. She didn't wait for an answer. "*If* there's a grotto inside the cliff – and I do mean *if*, Jason – there may be treasure. And *if* – and I'm not kidding about the *if*, Jason, so don't start thinking I totally believe you – *if* there is treasure, then maybe Ulysses Moore created some kind of treasure hunt."

"That's pretty far-fetched," Rick said.

"Do you have a better explanation?" Julia countered. "Is it really so crazy? Pirates used to hide treasure all the time. They made maps and stuff," she said. "Or at least, I think they did."

It was silent for a moment. Then, "I think you might be getting carried away," Rick said. "Let's take things one step at a time."

"*Boriiiiing*," Julia replied. "Come on, Rick. Use your imagination," she urged. "The message talks about a fleet, right? And to have a fleet, you've got to be a big-time fisherman or a pirate. And if you're a pirate, you've probably got treasure."

Rick was not at all convinced by Julia's reasoning. But he bit his tongue. There was no point in arguing with her. Besides, it *was* an intriguing idea. . .

"Jason thinks the message was written by Ulysses,"

Julia continued. "I say he did it to lead us to treasure! Let's imagine that there's a grotto inside the cliff. All we've got to do is figure out the earthlights . . . and how we can get *inside* the grotto."

"If I'm right about Ulysses Moore," Jason said, "it seems reasonable to believe that he was able to get in and out of the grotto fairly easily."

"Maybe," Rick conceded.

"I think the old man went down into the grotto from Argo Manor," Jason said. "And I think I know how he did it."

"You guys are nuts," Rick exclaimed. "It's one wild guess after another with you two. But go on, I'm listening. Please tell us, Jason: how did he do it?"

Jason triumphantly pointed to the hulking wardrobe that stood against the wall.

"There's a secret door behind there," Jason informed them. "If you give me a hand moving that thing, you can see it for yourselves."

The door was intimidating. Or, in Julia's words, "downright creepy".

In many ways, it was no different from any other door in the house. It was just a door. But there was something unusual about it. It was old, for one thing. The wood was covered with scratches and deep gashes, as if the door had been struck with dozens of blows.

They studied it for a long time. They had to work very hard to move the heavy wardrobe enough to reveal the whole thing. It seemed that the piece of furniture had been placed there with the intention of blocking it. And now that it had been revealed, that intention made the door even more fascinating.

Every instinct in Jason's body told him they had to open that door.

"You think this is it?" Julia asked.

Jason had picked up the map of the house. He marked an *X* on the spot where the door was located. "Definitely. This is it," Jason announced. "This is one of the secret doors old Ulysses uses to sneak around."

"Jason!" his sister said. "Will you stop it with that stuff? Ulysses Moore is DEAD."

"What makes you so sure?" Jason challenged. "I saw him!"

Rick and Julia stared at him.

"What do you mean?" Rick asked. "You saw a ghost? Or you saw the real, living man?"

"When I came down to get the pen," Jason answered. "It was only for a second, but I saw a glimpse of a shifting shadow. Then he was gone."

Jason looked first at Rick, then at his sister. Their expressions were of disbelief and disapproval. "You don't believe me, do you?" he asked.

Julia paced across the room, running her hands through her hair. "I'm such an idiot!" she exclaimed. "This is how you saw the grotto, too, isn't it?" she accused Jason.

"So?" Jason answered.

"I can't believe I was such a sucker," she fumed. "The grotto, the hollow cliff, the secret passageway behind this door – you made it all up! You didn't really see a grotto! You just imagined it!"

"No!" Jason pleaded. "I saw it!"

Julia looked her brother squarely in the eye. "Swear it," she said angrily. "Swear to me that you saw a grotto."

Jason felt his face grow flushed. He closed his eyes and pictured what he had seen when he was dangling from the cliff.

It had been an empty space.

No.

He didn't see it. He *sensed* a vast space.

No, in truth, not even that.

He'd sensed . . . *something.* Like there might be a space behind the cliff. It was a feeling. But everything in his heart told Jason to trust that feeling.

Even so, doubt crept into his mind. He hadn't

truly seen a grotto. Just as, he had to admit, he hadn't truly seen the shadow of Ulysses Moore.

"Jason?" Rick said. His voice sounded far away. "Are you OK?"

Jason looked around the room, tired and defeated. "No," he confessed. "I can't swear that I saw anything."

Julia turned her back on him angrily.

Rick looked at each twin. Julia was furious, that much was obvious. And Jason? Well, he looked nervous. But at the same time, he was defiant. As if he knew he was right.

"It's not that important what you saw or didn't see. Let's stick with what's real," Rick said at last. "Are you listening, Julia?"

Without turning around, she nodded yes.

"We know that this box really exists," Rick said, holding it up. "It is real. And the message is real, too. No one imagined this. No one made it up. It's right here."

He handed the parchment to Julia. She turned to face the two boys.

Rick pointed to the door. "And that door," he said, "is very, very real."

Julia looked at him, then Jason, and relented. "So, let's open it!"

*   *   *

Since the door had no handle or knob, Julia tried slipping her finger into what seemed to be a keyhole. She tried pushing, pulling, and wiggling it around. Nothing worked.

"It's shut solid," she groaned.

Jason slowly ran his hand over the ancient door, as if probing for secrets. He knelt before the key-hole that Julia had jiggled with her finger. "It's like a puzzle. A door that can't be opened."

"Well, why can't a door be opened?" Rick asked himself aloud. "The answer is simple. It must be locked." He pointed to a series of holes in the door. "And that must be how we unlock it."

Julia leaned closer. On the left half of the door, there were four keyholes, positioned crosswise, like the angles of a diamond.

"Not one key but four!" Julia sighed. "Could this be any more complicated?"

"We could try talking to Nestor," Jason suggested.

"Or search the house, centimetre by centimetre, drawer by drawer, hoping we'll find the keys," Rick offered.

"That would take for ever!" Julia cried. She was beginning to despair of ever getting past the door when suddenly there was a gust of wind. A loud thump came from upstairs.

"It's him!" Jason exclaimed. He leaped to his feet.

They raced up the stairs and into the tower room – only to face more disappointment. It was just the window, once again banging against the frame of the old sill. Rick slammed it shut. "The latch is loose."

"That window didn't open by itself," Jason murmured. He searched the room with his eyes. "Somebody, or something, wanted us. This window is his signal for us to come up here." He gestured to the model sailing ships that were arranged on the desk. "Were these like this before?" he asked the others. "Do you remember? It looks like they've been moved."

Julia shrugged. "Search me."

The lead ship in the miniature fleet was resting on top of a slender book with a dark leather cover. The model was long and tapered, its framework made of dozens of tiny sticks held together by glue and thread.

Rick was unsure. None of them had noticed the book on their last visit to the tower. But they had left so quickly, racing after Julia to go for a swim, that it was hard to be certain. "It may have been here," Rick said. "I don't remember it, but . . . well, that's the only logical explanation: we didn't notice it before."

Jason picked up the miniature ship and placed it in Rick's hands. Rick read the small copper plaque on its base: "*Nefertiti's Eye*," he said. "That must be the name of the ship."

Rick turned the model over in his hands. "It looks Egyptian. I bet these sticks are papyrus."

Jason opened up the small, handsome journal that had served as the ship's pedestal. It was a diary. Someone had jotted down notes and comments in a tiny scrawl that was difficult to read. The journal was filled with drawings and scraps of paper.

"Egypt," Jason said, with slight disappointment. "This is some kind of travel diary about a trip to Egypt." He thumbed through the pages. There were hieroglyphs, a drawing of the golden mask of the child pharaoh Tutankhamen, a sculpture of the head of his mother, Nefertiti, a map of the Valley of the Kings where Tutankhamen's great treasure had been discovered, and much more.

"This diary is mostly about Tutankhamen," he told Julia and Rick. "It's full of drawings, underlined words, notes, things circled in red. Weird."

He continued reading through the pages. "Hmm. Ulysses Moore kept a list of Egyptian building materials in this diary. He must have been fascinated by their lost culture."

Rick raised the ship in his hands. "He must have been really meticulous when he made his models, like he needed them to be exactly perfect."

Julia placed her hand on Jason's arm. "Wait a minute," she whispered. "This might be the fleet mentioned in the message. *The fleet that takes you where you choose.* It could be his way of saying that . . . that with these models he could travel to different places and times and, you know, go anywhere in his imagination." She turned to Rick. "Don't you think?"

Rick nodded. "Maybe, but it seems too simple. We found this message hidden inside a cliff, remember? And what about the earth-lights?"

"Hey, what's this?" Jason interrupted. He had turned a page and found what looked like a receipt of some kind. It definitely wasn't from ancient Egypt.

Rick looked at it over Jason's shoulder. "*Post Office, Kilmore Cove,*" he read aloud.

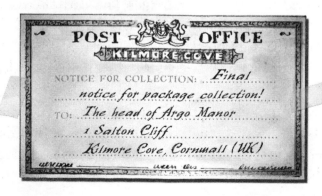

"This should be enough to convince you that old Ulysses is dead," Julia said to her brother. "He never got the chance to pick up his package."

But nothing could shake Jason's faith. "Maybe he left it here for us," he said excitedly. "The window banging, the diary, the postal slip neatly tucked inside – maybe none of this is an accident."

Julia made a face. "Look, Jason. For all we know, the diary could have been beneath that model the whole time. Don't start getting spooky on us again."

"We have to get this package!" Jason blurted. He was determined.

"Today is Saturday," Julia said. "The post office won't be open. We don't live in the city any more, Jason, in case you haven't noticed. We're lucky Kilmore Cove even *has* a post office."

Rick tilted his head from side to side. "Small towns do have their advantages," he said. "Around here, if people know who you are, they'll go out of their way to do you a favour. We can try Ms Calypso's bookshop. She runs the post office, too."

"Do you know her?" Jason asked.

Rick grinned. "Are you kidding? In this town, everyone knows everybody."

"One big happy family," Julia mumbled, "like the Simpsons."

Jason bounced on the balls of his feet. "Do you really think she would open the post office for us?"

"No harm in asking," Rick said.

"Guys, chill," Julia protested. "What about the door? The secret grotto? The mysterious message? Suddenly that's not fun any more? Now you want to go to the post office instead?"

Jason and Rick weren't listening. They were already halfway down the stairs.

"Is it just me," Julia muttered to herself, "or does this all seem really stupid?" Then she brushed the hair from her face and raced after the boys. Stupid or not, she wasn't about to sit around while they had all the fun.

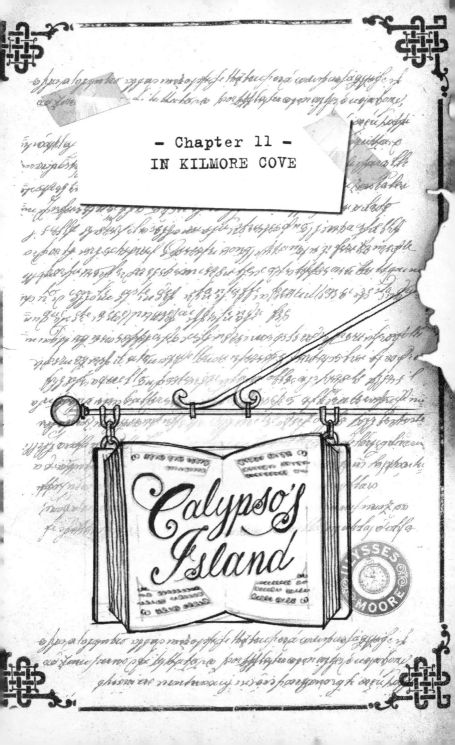

Calypso's Island

It was late in the afternoon, but still well before dinner, when Nestor opened the door to Argo Manor's garage for the two boys. The door rose with a squeak, revealing a dusty place that was poorly lit by a single light bulb hanging from the ceiling. Most of the garage was taken up by the shape of a car covered with a white sheet. Rick couldn't resist peeking underneath. He saw a classic roadster from the 1950s.

Nestor winked. "A toy," he commented.

"Does she still run?" Rick asked, admiring the car.

"Very doubtful," Nestor replied. "Many years have passed since anyone drove it."

Nestor walked around the car to the back of the garage. "Aha, yes, here it is." He lifted up a sheet to uncover a bicycle – a very old, very heavy bicycle, Rick noted in disappointment.

Rick grabbed the handlebars and wheeled the bicycle out of the garage. Since his bike had been damaged by Oblivia Newton's car, he had no choice but to borrow this one from Nestor. He had hoped for something better than a rusty pile of junk, though.

"This thing looks older than you," Rick joked to Nestor.

"It still gets the job done," Nestor retorted. "Don't let looks deceive you."

Rick lifted the bike a few centimetres off the ground, feeling its heft. No gears, he noted. Man, this was going to be a killer to pedal back up to the house. But in a way, he was looking forward to the challenge.

Jason and Julia, of course, had their own bikes. Newer, lighter, faster. It would be a job to keep up with them.

Nestor thrust a tyre pump into Rick's hands. He handed Jason an oil can and a rag. "Get on with it, then," he said.

Jason looked at the bike doubtfully. "Are you sure you'll be able to ride this to town and back?" he asked Rick. "Maybe this isn't such a good idea."

"The bike is old, but sturdy," Nestor interrupted. "It will be fine. As for coming back up the hill, the bicycle will do its job. The question is if Rick has the muscles – and the heart – for it."

"Don't worry about me," Rick said. He bent down and rapidly pumped air into the tyres. Nestor glanced at him approvingly.

"Might I ask why you're going into town at this hour?" he asked the boys.

Jason knitted his brows briefly, a telltale sign of his discomfort. "No reason," he answered. "We just felt like cruising around, maybe getting some chocolate."

"Not too much junk food," Nestor warned them. "When you return, I'll have dinner warming on the stove. Have a good time."

Minutes later, Rick was ready. Julia and Jason were on their bikes, waiting by the gate. They waved to Nestor and headed down the steep winding road that led into town and the bay of Kilmore Cove.

Julia shot out ahead, her hair flying beneath her helmet. She took the first turn hard, leaning into it at a sharp angle, shouting happily. "Slow down," Jason called out in protest, but then he, too, plummeted down the curving road. Rick pedalled slowly behind them, testing the brakes as he went. He turned his head one last time towards the great house on the cliff.

Nestor was there, shielding his eyes from the sun. He watched the three disappear down the road. "Who knows?" he murmured to himself. "Maybe they will surprise us after all."

The downhill ride was exhilarating. Their wheels spun effortlessly as the town came into view bit by bit, hairpin turn after hairpin turn. Kilmore Cove was a cluster of small houses painted many different colours huddled together in the most protected part of the bay. The seashore road was intersected by small connecting roads that led away from the water, forming a series of T's beside the sea.

Cars crowded the narrow streets as their drivers searched for parking spaces along the harbour. People passed each other and smiled on the promenade, the salt air filling their lungs.

Julia was the first to arrive. She jumped off her bike and leaned it against a road sign. The sign advised drivers not to park too close to the beach because the tide might carry off their cars. Julia wasn't sure if the sign was a joke or not.

"Hey! I beat you, slug!" she yelled as Jason pulled up beside her.

Finally, Rick cruised his bike down the last stretch of road. He didn't mind being last – he was just grateful he'd made it in one piece.

"So where do we find Ms Calypso?" Julia asked impatiently.

Rick led the way, pushing the rugged, thick-tyred bicycle in front of him. They moved deeper into the heart of town, passing a statue of a sailor standing proudly with one foot on an anchor – a tribute to the town's seafaring heritage. They came to a beautiful fountain made of ancient stones. The water sparkled in the sunlight.

"In here," Rick gestured.

He pointed to the wooden sign:

CALYPSO'S ISLAND
Fine Books Saved from the Sea, New and Used

Rick pushed the door open. A little bell over the doorway let out a cheerful jingle.

It was an old-fashioned bookshop, quite unlike the vast, clean, uncluttered mega-stores that Julia and Jason knew back in London. Books were stacked on the ground and on low wooden shelves that formed a sort of pathway through the shop. It was a maze – a labyrinth of books.

"Just a second!" a voice called out from around the corner.

Ms Calypso was a petite woman with clear eyes and a calm demeanour. She was wearing a large silk scarf and a long flowery dress. A pair of practical flat shoes completed her outfit.

"Rick Banner! What a pleasant surprise." She paused, glancing warmly at Julia and Jason. "You two must be the Londoners."

They exchanged greetings and shook hands.

"It's a good sign to see you in the bookshop so soon after moving here," Ms Calypso noted with a wink. "Business has been slow. I need all the readers I can get."

Ms Calypso leaned forward, placing a hand on Jason's shoulder. She whispered, "And what do you think of Kilmore Cove? Is it too small? Too remote? Too stuck in the middle of nowhere?"

"Oh no," Jason replied.

"Of course," Ms Calypso pressed on, "it must come as a great shock for you, to move from Piccadilly Circus to our sea-swept rocks and the far-flung shores. From Big Ben to our little lighthouse. Except that, after all, you do live in Argo Manor. And when one lives in a house like that," she said, "well, what a paradise! The sea, the sky, the great old house. Who could ask for more?"

Rick stood by in silence, politely waiting for a chance to speak. "Actually, we came here on business," he said.

"Of course!" Ms Calypso exclaimed. "You need books!" She flicked a hand at the bookshelves. "It's a small shop, but well stocked. Sports, mystery, history, magic, religion, literature – whatever your interests, I probably have a book for you!"

Julia glanced quickly at Jason and Rick. She sensed that it was up to her. "Actually," Julia said, "we didn't come here for a book."

"No?" Ms Calypso looked into Julia's eyes. "Then what brings you to me?"

Jason handed Ms Calypso the slip they had found

at Argo Manor. She took it from him, frowning slightly. "Who gave you this?" she asked sharply.

"The old caretaker, Nestor," Jason lied with surprising ease. "He told us to come here and see if you could get the package for us." He paused, then added, "Please."

Ms Calypso seemed to think it over. "It is Saturday," she stated. "The post office is closed."

"Oh, please," Jason pleaded. "If you'd be kind enough to open it for just a minute, we'd be so grateful."

Ms Calypso shook her head. "Even if the office were open, I couldn't give you what you seek. The delivery slip says that it's to be given only to 'The Head of Argo Manor'. All I see before me are three children."

Jason and Julia explained that their parents were the heads of Argo Manor. Jason nodded, adding, "At the moment they're too busy with our move. Otherwise they would have come to pick it up themselves."

"Nestor said that you would understand," Julia added.

Ms Calypso shrugged and relented. "Oh well, why not? It's typical of the owner of Argo Manor to send someone to run his errands."

"Then you'll open up the post office?" Julia asked.

"No," Ms Calypso answered, her lips curled up in a feline smile. "It is Saturday! And rules should always be obeyed – don't you agree?"

"Three books."

Ms Calypso turned to look at Rick. He stood ramrod straight, as if challenging Ms Calypso to a duel.

"I beg your pardon, Rick?" she said.

"If you open the post office for my friends," he said, "then we will buy and read three books. You can choose them yourself." In his pocket, he had the money that Manfred, the chauffeur, had given him.

A slight smile formed on Ms Calypso's face. She was clearly intrigued by Rick's offer. "Three books," she mused. She glanced towards the cash register. "Well, it has been a bad month for business and the rent is due."

"Please," Julia urged.

Ms Calypso held out her hand. Her grip was strong. "It's a deal," she agreed, shaking on it.

Fifteen minutes later, Jason, Julia, and Rick found themselves on the very edge of a jetty stretching out into the sea. The cliff towered up to their left. The harbour, full of battered fishing boats, was to their right.

Jason held a package about the size of a shoebox wrapped in brown packing tape. Julia unhappily shifted the bulk of three hardback books in her arms. "It was your brilliant idea, Rick," she grumbled. "You hold them." She thrust the books into his hands.

Rick smiled at Julia. "Hey, it worked, didn't it?" He glanced at the titles. Ms Calypso had selected *Wuthering Heights* for Julia. For him, it was Jules Verne's *The Mysterious Island*. But poor Jason had the thickest, most intimidating book of all – *Ramses* by Christian Jacq.

Jason slowly, patiently peeled the tape off the package.

"Look!" he cried, beaming.

Inside the box, buried beneath a cushion of crumpled newspaper, were four keys.

The keys were very old, very ornate, and covered with a thin film of red dust. Each key had a finely crafted handle. Rick picked up one at random, raising it into the light for a better look.

"It's an animal," he murmured, studying the carved handle.

Julia leaned into Rick's shoulder. "You're right," she whispered. "Is it a lizard?"

Jason had picked up another one. "I'd say that this one is a hedgehog or a porcupine," he announced.

Julia chose a key with a handle in the shape of an elephant.

"Hey, it even looks like you," Jason teased.

"Ha-ha, very clever," Julia replied sarcastically. "You sooooo slay me with your wit, Jason. You compare me to an elephant – but you forget that I'm your twin!"

The final key was a bird with the face of an owl. "Lizard, hedgehog, elephant, and owl," Rick murmured, studying the four keys. "What do these animals have in common?"

Julia shrugged. "I don't know, a love of romantic films and long walks on the beach?"

"Get serious for once," Jason replied sharply. "Can't you see? At Argo Manor we have a door with four locks. And here, by some crazy stroke of luck, four keys have been handed to us!"

"Freaky," Julia commented.

"Is there anything else in the box?" Rick asked.

Jason searched through the pieces of newspaper. He lifted out a rolled-up parchment similar to the one they had found inside the cliff. The parchment was covered with the same symbols as the message from the cliff.

"Freaky deaky," Julia said.

"*Now* do you guys believe me?" Jason asked. "There's something weird going on at Argo Manor. Ulysses Moore had secrets. And we're going to get to the bottom of them."

- Chapter 12 -
A SUDDEN STORM

The three children began the long, arduous climb back up to Argo Manor. Having lived all his life by the steep cliffs of Kilmore Cove, Rick was prepared for the challenge – even with Nestor's old, heavy bike. *Just grind it out, one pedal after another,* he told himself. *Don't look around, don't fret, just keep those legs steadily churning.*

Rick wondered how the twins would manage. Even with superior bicycles, they would probably have a hard time making it to the top. He smiled to himself when Julia raced into the lead. *She'll never be able to keep it up,* he thought.

Rick matched pace with Jason, who was riding just off to his right. Up they climbed, up and up. Rick could sense Jason faltering, a pained expression on his face. Jason's breathing became heavier. His weight shifted awkwardly.

Yet, Rick noted, Jason refused to give up.

Ahead, there was still no sign of Julia. Rick was impressed. But even though Jason could not match his sister's ability, Rick saw that he had heart.

"Let's rest," Rick finally said. He pulled to the side of the road and dismounted. It was an act of kindness towards Jason, who quickly accepted the suggestion. He stood bent over the bike frame, struggling to catch his breath. "Wow," he said at last.

Rick smiled.

"My heart is pounding," Jason confessed.

"Let's walk the rest of the way," Rick suggested. "It's not that far."

The two boys strode the long road together. Their bodies ached, yet their minds raced with possibilities. The secret door, the strange keys, the mysteries of Ulysses Moore!

"We're almost home," Jason said after a while.

And at that instant the clouds burst with rain. It was a sudden, violent downpour. In seconds, the boys were drenched.

"Nice weather we're having," Jason commented in a flat, matter-of-fact tone.

Rick shook his head and laughed. Soon Jason joined in. The two boys felt giddy, laughing in the rain.

A crackling fire awaited them inside the house. A dry Julia – she had managed to beat the rain – greeted them with a smile. She threw a change of clothes into Rick's arms "They're my dad's," she said. "It may not do much for your street cred, but at least you won't be wet."

Nestor was in the kitchen, clanging pots.

"He's making soup," Julia told the boys. "Dinner is almost ready."

Jason glanced at Rick. "Don't say anything about the keys in front of Nestor," he warned.

"Why not?" Rick asked.

"I can't say exactly," Jason replied. "Just a feeling, I suppose."

"I don't totally trust him, either," Julia said. "Let's keep this to ourselves for now."

They gathered around the kitchen table a few minutes later. Nestor whistled happily while stirring the soup on the stove. Rain drummed against the windowpanes. The fire crackled in the fireplace, filling the rooms with a warm, smoky aroma.

The telephone rang. It was Jason and Julia's parents, checking in.

"Yes, yes, everything's fine," Jason said. He neglected to mention the small detail that he'd almost fallen off the cliff and died a horrible death.

His mother asked to speak to Nestor.

The old man looked at the three children as he spoke into the phone. He winked and stirred the soup with his free hand. "Three angels," the caretaker said into the phone. "No problem at all. Of course. Yes, yes, yes. Don't worry about a thing. No, of course not. No problem. Vegetable soup. With fresh bread." He made a face. "Yes, I'll make sure they brush their teeth. All right. Enjoy yourselves. Everything's fine. Take as long as you need."

Nestor handed the phone to Julia. "Your turn," he whispered.

Jason could barely contain himself during dinner. He had four keys burning a hole in his pocket. Yet they couldn't be used until Nestor left them alone. "We'll clean up," he finally offered. "You've already done so much for us."

Nestor nodded and pushed himself away from the table. "Perhaps Mr Banner would like to spend the night," he suggested. "It's raining awfully hard outside."

Rick's heart leaped. "I'd love to!" he exclaimed. "I mean, sure, if it's OK with these guys."

Rick phoned home, and it was settled. He was to spend the night at Argo Manor. A peal of thunder cracked through the air, and the house lights flickered for a moment. Nestor looked distractedly at the lights, which dimmed and then brightened again. He rose and turned to leave.

"Where are you going?" Julia asked.

Nestor placed his hand on the doorknob and turned it with a decisive *clack*. "Back to my house. No offence, but I am an old man and I prefer to spend my time alone with a book. You will be fine. You know where I am if you need anything."

He pointed to the dishwasher. "The detergent is

in that bottom cupboard," he said. "Do a good job cleaning up."

With that, he walked out into the storm.

- Chapter 13 -
A FACE IN THE WINDOW

Within minutes, Jason had slammed the bulky *Dictionary of Forgotten Languages* on the kitchen table. Rick quickly cleared the dishes. Julia puzzled over the parchment. "I thought he'd never leave," she commented.

"But you have to admit that soup hit the spot," Rick countered.

Jason didn't reply. He was lost in the book. Once again, he was in the same room with Rick and Julia, yet his mind was a million miles away.

From inside the caretaker's quarters, Nestor looked across the dark courtyard to the lights of Argo Manor's kitchen. He smiled. Argo Manor had come back to life.

"Just like old times," he said softly. Living alone had given him the habit of thinking out loud. In truth, Nestor hoped that, with those children there, things would be even better than they'd been in the old times. He thought back to early that afternoon and his visit from Oblivia Newton. His teeth clenched involuntarily.

"You'll never get this house, Oblivia," he whispered.

He stood for a long time, thinking about Oblivia's ruthless attempts to take Argo Manor. And yet he could not help remembering about the twins and Rick inside the house. They seemed to be her opposite in every way. They were open while Oblivia was closed. They had imagination and intelligence while Oblivia knew only greed and money and lust for power. Jason, Rick, and Julia, Nestor decided, represented youth and hope. Oblivia could bring only ruin and despair.

Oblivia Newton had tried to get her hands on Argo Manor in every legal way possible. She had offered huge amounts of money. "Ask for anything you'd like," she had told the owner. "I'll give it to you."

"Fine," Ulysses Moore had told her. "I want you to go away."

This only insulted Oblivia – and unfortunately, made her even more determined to get Argo Manor. No matter what it took.

The storm crashed down with increasing intensity. Argo Manor began to creak and groan, as if the house itself was protesting.

In the kitchen, Julia, Jason, and Rick huddled together, reading the translation of their latest parchment out loud. And while the first message had been mysterious, this second clue seemed completely incomprehensible:

*"While of four one will open by lot
Of four three the motto will show
Of four two mean death on the spot
And one of four will lead below."*

Julia summed up their feelings in her own unique style: "This is rubbish," she concluded.

Rick kept trying to figure it out by applying practical logic. "OK," he began, "we can't be sure that the first message is really the first message."

"Huh?" Julia grunted.

Rick explained, "I mean, we were likely to find this second message more quickly – more easily than the one in the cliff. So it might be that the second message is really the first. Even if our hunch is right, that we're on some sort of crazy treasure hunt, we can't be sure we're actually beginning at the beginning. So let's get back to basics," he continued. "Here's what we do know: we have four keys in our hands."

Julia chimed in, "And on this parchment it says that *of four one will open by lot* – blah, blah, blah. My guess is that *one* is the door over there. And *lot* could mean more of them, like 'a whole lot'."

Rick shrugged, unconvinced. "It might be *one* of the keys," he countered. "Since *by lot* means by chance or luck."

"Like a lottery," Julia added.

"Like destiny," Jason said. His voice seemed far away. It was the first thing he'd said since Nestor left. "A *lot* can mean our fate," he said. "It may be our lot in life to open that door."

Julia cast a worried look at her twin. Jason simply . . . believed. He believed that it wasn't an accident that he'd been dangling from that cliff. It wasn't chance. It wasn't luck, either.

This was destiny taking over.

Jason felt it. He knew. As if some unseen hand were guiding him, leading him and the others to some unknown task. And sometimes his belief in things like destiny and fate freaked his sister out.

Jason left the others in the kitchen. Everybody needed a break. He made his way towards the stone room without turning on the lights. He crossed through two sitting rooms, which, in the dark, seemed especially eerie. The furniture in the rooms looked like sleeping figures. The rain and the wind had grown in intensity, howling to the point that it seemed like the house was on the verge of being blown down the cliff. The tower at the top of the stairs groaned in the wind. The night itself was wild, like a raging beast, clawing at whatever stood in its way.

Jason had the four keys with him. He felt their

weight in the pockets of his trousers. He fished them out and held them tightly as he stepped slowly, deliberately, towards his destination. When he reached the stone room, it was very dark. Jason groped for the light switch.

A flash of lightning suddenly cut through the darkness, and Jason saw something outside the window.

It was a face. Two eyes.

Two eyes staring at him.

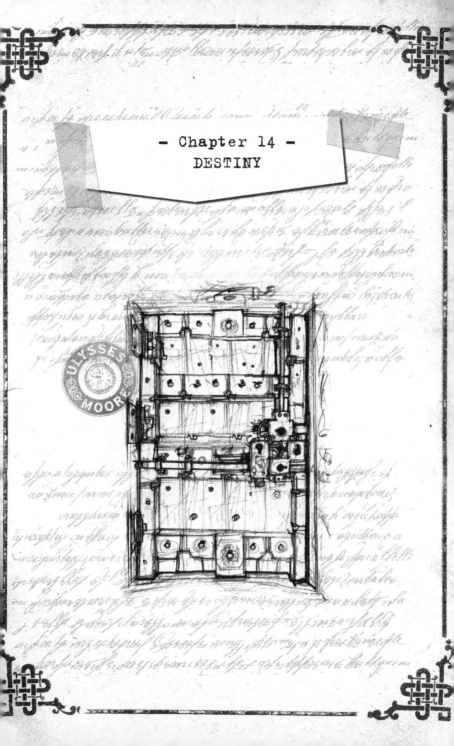

- Chapter 14 -
DESTINY

Rick and Julia rushed to the source of Jason's cry. They found him in the darkness of the stone room. He was pointing at the window.

"He's here," Jason intoned. "He's out there."

"Who? Who is here?" Rick asked urgently.

"Calm down, Jason," Julia said to her twin. "Turn on a light," she told Rick.

Rick flicked it on. "What did you see?" Rick asked. "Tell us exactly what you saw."

"The lightning flashed," Jason said. "There was a face, the face of a man, hovering outside the window. Staring in at me."

One thing was clear to both Julia and Rick: Jason had no doubt about the truth of his story. Even if they found it hard to believe, Jason himself was absolutely positive.

"Are you sure it was a man?" Rick asked.

Jason nodded, still in a state of shock. "Yes, a man."

"Are all the doors locked?" Julia asked.

In a flash, Rick raced through the house, checking and double-checking each door and window. He turned on every light he could find. "Everything's locked tight," he announced when he returned.

Jason had calmed down. He was sitting quietly, his sister beside him.

"It was the ghost of Ulysses Moore," Jason told them. He stared into Rick's eyes almost pleadingly. "You've got to believe me, Rick. The face was horrible, with a scar that went all the way across it."

"Shhh, Jason," Julia whispered. "We're safe here. We're all together. The house is locked. Nestor isn't far away."

Jason fidgeted with the four keys in his hands. Lizard, hedgehog, elephant, owl. "What about up there?" he asked with a tremulous voice.

He meant, of course, the room at the top of the tower. The room with the diary. The fleet of ships.

There was a violent boom, a flash of lightning, and the electricity went out altogether.

"Oh great," Julia said under her breath.

"It will come back on in a second," Rick said. "Don't be afraid."

"You hear that? Did you hear it?" Jason stood up again.

"Did we hear what, Jason?" Julia managed to answer in the darkness. She reached for Jason's hands and squeezed.

Jason did not answer.

Because now Julia heard it, too.

It was the wind.

It was the rain.

It was the dark threat of the night.

It was the window up in the tower, slamming against its frame, banging rhythmically.

Like footsteps.

For the first time in a long time, Julia wished that her mother and father were home.

Rick's face suddenly glowed in the darkness. "It's my lighter," he explained. "My father always said it's a good idea to keep one on you at all times."

He slowly moved away from the twins. "I'll go and close the window upstairs."

"No!" Julia cried.

"Why not?"

"Stay here," Julia ordered. "Let's all just stay here until the lights come back on. What do you say, huh?"

"It's just a storm," Rick said. "There's no point in sitting around whimpering in the dark." He paused, flicking his lighter. "Are there any candles around here? A torch? Anything?"

"I think I remember seeing candles in one of the kitchen drawers," Julia answered.

"OK," Rick said calmly. "That's good, right? I'll go and get them."

But Julia decided that it would be best if they all went together. So they did. Rick led the way, flicking his lighter for a few seconds at a time before it became too hot for his fingers. Each flash gave them just enough light to get their bearings. They weaved their way half-blind through the darkened rooms – seeing, unseeing, seeing, unseeing, slowly making their way through the dark.

When they reached the kitchen the electricity came back on just as suddenly as it had gone out. Every corner of Argo Manor was lit once more. But the children stuffed candles in their pockets just in case. Then they climbed the stairs to the tower together. Rick closed the window again.

As they headed back down the stairs, Rick asked, "Did you guys notice how many windows there are in the tower?"

"Nope," Julia replied.

"Four," Rick said. "One on each side."

Jason added, "*While of four one will open by lot.* That could mean the windows! Just like I read in my book – a spirit is trying to communicate with us, using that open window!"

Rick shook his head. "No. I don't think so. The word four must refer to the four keys. While one . . . one is. . ."

"Destiny," Julia said, completing his thought.

* * *

They returned to the stone room. Jason could not help glancing at the window, wondering if the face might appear again. But the presence of his sister and Rick calmed him, and soon all three children were studying the four locks in the door. There were four circular holes, all identical, arranged like this:

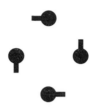

There was no indication of which key fitted which lock.

"All this thinking is getting us nowhere," Julia complained. "Let's just try them randomly."

"No," Rick said. "There has to be a logical pattern here. We just haven't recognized it yet. Lizard, hedgehog, elephant, owl. What do these animals have in common?"

"Not this again," Julia groaned.

"The message says *by lot*," Jason reminded the others.

"I understand what the message says," Rick replied. He was losing patience. "But we have to at least come up with a plan!"

"Here's a plan," Julia replied. "Let's start shoving keys in the locks and see if we get lucky."

"But what if we end up ruining some kind of mechanism?" Rick protested. "There might be only one chance of getting to the treasure."

Julia and Jason thought about that. Rick had a point.

"Let's try with the elephant on top," Jason said.

"Okaaay," Julia said. "Why not the hedgehog?"

"*E* is for elephant," Jason said. "It's the first letter in alphabetical order."

"Then where do we put the lizard?" Rick asked. "In the lock on the left or the one on the right?"

Jason didn't answer. He had no idea.

"And what if we're using the wrong names?" Rick questioned. "This one seems more like a newt than a lizard."

"A newt?!" scoffed Julia. "A *newt*?! Don't tell me you know the difference between a newt and a lizard."

Rick narrowed his eyes, uncertain how to take Julia's comments. "Look," he replied. He ran his finger along the carved animal. "It has a small tail and smooth skin, not scales."

"Wow," Julia said with what seemed like genuine respect. "You really do know the difference between a newt and a lizard. I'm impressed. But what about the others? Do you know what kind of owl this is?"

Rick shrugged, smiling shyly. "Just an owl."

Jason handed him another key. "This is definitely a porcupine, not a hedgehog," he said.

"Why?"

"Porcupines are chubby," Jason said with earnestness. "But hedgehogs are more like mice. And they have pointy noses. This is definitely a porcupine."

No one could argue with that. Probably because everyone was tired of arguing.

All that was left was the elephant. African or Indian – it didn't seem to make much difference. Plain old elephant seemed good enough. Julia attempted a new line of reasoning. "If the owl eats the newt," she began.

"Owls don't eat newts," Rick stated.

"The elephant could stamp on all of the others," Julia said. "But he'd have to be careful with the porcupine!"

"You're just being ridiculous, Julia," Jason scolded. "Can't you be serious?"

Next they considered the geographical regions in which each animal lived. The top lock could be north and the bottom south. West was left, east was right.

"Porcupines are primarily from the Americas," Rick reasoned. "West. The lock on the left."

"But owls live all over the place," Julia pointed out. "This isn't going to work."

They tried sizes, then colours. But no matter how hard they tried, they couldn't find a logical connection between the four keys.

Finally, Julia lost her patience. She grabbed the owl key and slipped it into the uppermost lock on the door.

"Wait!" cried Rick.

Julia turned the key. *Click.*

"You see!" Julia exclaimed triumphantly. "Easy as pie!"

"How did you do that?!" Jason asked, astonished.

Julia grinned. "I put it in and turned it. I guess that makes me a genius. Now hand me the others."

"Which one next?" Jason asked.

"Elephant," Julia decided.

She slowly slid it into the lock on the left and gave it a turn.

Click.

"Porcupine!" Julia ordered.

Clack.

"Newt."

Julia took the last key from Jason and inserted it into the bottom lock of the diamond pattern. Once again, the key turned easily.

Clack.

Julia smiled, thoroughly pleased with herself. "Done," Julia said. "Thank you, ladies and gentlemen. Please send your cards and prizes to Argo Manor, care of Julia Covenant."

"Not so fast, genius," Rick chided. He placed one hand on the door and pushed it.

It didn't budge.

Rick grabbed one of the keys and tugged on it a little. "I'm just a simple guy, Julia," he said. "I've never lived in the big city or anything. But something tells me this door is still locked."

Julia was overcome by a wave of disappointment. She gave the owl key a second and then a third twist.

Click, click.

"They're just turning without doing anything," she realized.

She tried turning them each four times.

And then twice again. Angrily.

The door remained closed.

Rick looked at Julia seriously. "See? There's got to be a rule for unlocking this door. There has to be a logical way of working it out."

Jason turned to the door and raised his arms above his head. "Open up!" he shouted. "Open up!" He banged his fists against the wood. His thumps echoed back eerily.

Jason turned to Rick and Julia, his eyes gleaming. "Did you hear that?" he said with excitement. "It's empty back there."

Jason and Julia shifted the keys around in the various patterns, turning them with no success. Rick picked up the translation of the parchment and began to study it line by line.

"*Of four three the motto will show.* What motto?" he wondered. Rick continued to puzzle over the riddle: "*Of four two mean death on the spot.* Which of these animals means death? And which one leads below?"

While Rick racked his brain, Jason attempted to use a single key in each of the four locks. He would slide one in, turn it, take it out, and slide it into the next lock. As for the order of the locks he chose, he tried clockwise, counterclockwise, first above and then below. Then right, then left. But after countless attempts, the door still remained locked tight.

"Maybe it's a trick devised to drive us insane," Julia said. She was only half joking. "I'm not even sure this is a real door any more."

She slumped down beside Rick. "Maybe we need some magic words," she said. "Like, 'Open sesame bagels!'"

Rick gave a half-smile.

But that got Jason thinking. "Or maybe it's like *The Lord of the Rings*," he said. "You know that scene outside the mines: 'Say friend and enter.'"

Rick snapped to attention. "Wait a minute. What did you say?"

Jason looked at him quizzically. "Say friend and enter," he repeated. "Those are the Elvish words that Gandalf reads before the Moria Gate."

"No, not you, Jason," Rick said. "Julia! You said. . ."

"I said," Julia interrupted, "'Open sesame bagels.'"

"Open," Rick repeated in a whisper. "Open, open, open." He reread the translation aloud. "Could it be?" he wondered.

"Um, Rick," Julia coaxed. "Could it be that, like, you're not making any sense?"

Rick snatched at the keys. He bent down on his knees and lined them up on the floor. "It spells a word!" he exclaimed. "These are the letters: N for newt, O for owl, P for porcupine, E for elephant!"

"Nope," Julia said.

"Huh?"

"Nope," Julia repeated. "It spells nope. N-O-P-E."

Rick grinned, thrilled to his bones. "Not nope," he said, shifting the keys around. "O-P-E-N. Open!"

Jason nodded. "Yes, yes. That makes sense."

Rick leaped to his feet and began feeding the keys into the locks. He murmured to himself. "The riddle said *with four . . . by lot . . . OPEN!*"

He placed the final key into the door:

O

N   P

E

He turned it.

Click went the lock.

And the door swung slowly open.

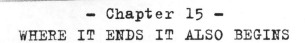

The three explorers stood motionless, silent, barely breathing.

The door was open.

Now what? It was as if they hadn't considered the possibility that they might actually succeed.

With their hearts in their mouths, the twins walked towards the door. It was massive and heavy, set into a sturdy frame. Beyond it they could make out a room that was dimly illuminated by the light from Argo Manor's stone room.

"What do we do now?" asked Julia, peering in with fascination.

"Let's check it out," Jason said.

Rick remained still, unwilling or unable to make a decision. Seeing that Jason was about to cross the threshold, Rick cried, "Wait! We can't go in there. We're not prepared."

Julia groaned. "We're not going on a camping trip," she told Rick. "We're just going to take a look around."

Rick shook his head. "It could be dangerous," he insisted. "We've got to think of everything we might need. Candles. The two parchments. The dictionary."

Julia resisted the urge to make another withering observation. Rick might be right. After all, he'd been the one to work out how to open the door.

"He's right," Jason said. "There might be more secret messages to figure out." He ran up to the tower room and grabbed the Egyptian diary and the box full of small clay balls.

Rick checked his lighter – it still worked – then dashed into the kitchen to get a knife. "I'd like to have some rope," he said. "Do you guys know where we can find some?"

"Oh, come on," Julia complained. "We're not climbing Mount Everest. Don't be such babies." With that, she turned her back on the boys and crossed through the door. Jason followed her.

The twins were swallowed up by the darkness. "Rick! Bring your lighter!" Jason called out. "We can't see anything in here!"

"I'm coming!" Rick shouted. "Don't take another step. There might be a well or who-knows-what in there!" Then he lit a candle and joined his friends.

The glow from the guttering flame gave the room an eerie, haunted quality, with shadows swaying on the walls, floor, and ceiling.

They were in a small, round room made entirely of stone. There were four stone archways, including the one they'd come through. The floor consisted of large, square blocks. It felt as if they were inside a medieval tower.

Rick used the flame from his candle to light two others. He handed the candles to Julia and Jason. They searched the room, looking for . . . well, they weren't sure exactly what they were looking for.

"Four pathways," Rick mused. "Four choices. Just like in the message."

Jason repeated some lines from memory:

> *"Of four three the motto will show*
> *Of four two mean death on the spot*
> *And one of four will lead below."*

"I can't say I'm crazy about that *death on the spot* part of the poem," Julia whispered.

Rick laughed softly. "No, we'll try to avoid that."

Jason was fixated on the last line. He murmured it aloud, running his hands along the walls: "*One of four will lead below.*"

"Look at this," Rick said suddenly. He drew their attention to animal figures that had been engraved on the stone archways that spanned the doors. "These look like a herd of charging bulls," Rick said.

"I suppose so," Jason said. "The engraving is so primitive, like it was done thousands of years ago."

"Here's a little school of fish," Julia announced. She pointed above another door. "What are those?"

"Moths," Rick stated. "Sphinx moths, to be accurate."

The expression on Julia's face was of utter disbelief. "Where do you come up with this stuff, Rick? Sphinx moths? What are you talking about?"

"Sphinx moths wake up when the sun goes down," Rick answered. "There's another name for them – hawk moths, I believe. Those black, hairy ones you see every once in a while."

Julia gave a grimace of disgust. "This archway has birds," she said.

"What kind of birds?" Rick asked.

Julia shrugged. "You're the expert on everything. *You* tell us."

Rick studied the engraving. "Albatrosses," he decided. "Wandering albatrosses."

Julia looked at Jason. "Where did you get this guy?"

"Rick does seem to know a lot of bizarre animal facts," Jason said with a laugh.

Rick raised his hands as if in apology. "It's interesting stuff!" he protested. "The albatross is a migratory seabird. They are called 'wandering' because sailors thought their cries sounded like the birds were lost at sea, crying out for home."

"Creepy," Julia said.

There was a persistent draught of air that made the candle flames flicker threateningly, forcing the children to move very slowly. As they made their way around the room, Jason noticed that a series of letters carved into the floor ran around the room's circumference.

"I think I've found the motto!" he called out happily. "Come and take a look!"

Jason bent down to the ground and brushed his hand over the letters carved in stone. Evenly spaced, they formed a single, very long line that curved around the room in a perfect circle.

"M-E-M-O-T," Jason began to read aloud. He moved slowly around the room, letter by letter. By the time he came full circle, everyone was completely confused.

"I don't understand a word of it," Julia said.

Neither did Jason or Rick. The message covered the circumference of the room, but it didn't seem to have a beginning or an end. It was just a series of letters that seemed impossible to understand.

"The motto is another riddle," Rick said. "Did you expect this to be easy? It's a secret message we're supposed to decipher. Like the one with the four keys. Like the one Jason found in the cliff."

"Well, yeah, sure," Julia said.

"ABIUSROMEMOT!" Jason shouted out in frustration, as he continued to read.

Julia looked at her brother and smiled.

"You know what?" she said happily. "Look at us. We're in the dark in a secret room in a house built on top of a cliff. There's a crazy storm outside and we have a secret message to decipher! And just think, I was afraid that I'd get bored in Kilmore Cove!"

Rick sat down in the centre of the room, dribbled a bit of melted wax on the ground, and stuck the candle firmly on top of it. He took out the sheet of paper on which they'd deciphered the other two messages, grabbed the pen, and asked Jason to read the letters aloud again.

"We can't go any further until we figure this out," Rick said. "We don't want to guess the wrong door and die on the spot. Right, Julia?"

Julia grinned. "Correctomundo, Rick."

Rick pointed behind them. "That's the door we came through. It's still there, and it's still open. We don't have to go any further if we aren't sure."

Jason and Julia nodded.

Jason began to dictate the letters. In the end the message read:

morsuibaabiusromemotepseespetome

"OK," Rick grumbled. "This is going to be harder than I thought."

"Let me see," Jason said. He sat down beside Rick and read the letters. He noticed that at one point of the message there were two *a*'s right next to each other.

"Let's try separating them," he said.

Rick drew a line between the two *a*'s.

morsuiba/abiusromemotepseespetome

Rick read, "*Morsuiba.* That sounds familiar."

"Don't tell me you speak Swahili, too," Julia said. She paused a beat. "You're joking, right?"

"No," Rick said earnestly. "I remember seeing this word in the dictionary."

Jason bounced up, excited. "Really?"

"I think so," Rick said. "Let's try to look it up."

Rick pulled the heavy dictionary on to his lap. He leafed through the pages of the oldest languages. Jason and Julia watched over his shoulder, fascinated.

"Here it is," Rick cried out triumphantly, pointing to a chapter of the dictionary entitled "The Language of the People of the Moon".

He read intently. "It says here that the word *suiba* means 'swift' or 'swiftly'."

"Let's try to translate the rest of it," Julia said.

"Hey!" Jason suddenly noticed. "You can read it both backwards and forwards. They're the same!"

"A palindrome," Julia whispered. Rick eyed her with a look of surprise. "Hey," she protested, "I pay attention at school sometimes."

Sure enough, by starting with the two *a*'s and reading the letters from left to right, the children found the word *Abiusrom*. And they read the same thing moving from right to left. But that wasn't all. Once they'd arrived at the end of the message, from both right and left, they could continue reading it starting at the other end, as if it were a ring.

As Julia had said, it was a palindrome. It could be read both backwards and forwards, without a beginning or an end. A magic sentence. A sentence that, at least at that moment, meant absolutely nothing to Jason, Julia, and Rick.

While Rick and Julia took a brief rest, Jason threw himself wholeheartedly into translating the message from the so-called language of the People of the Moon, whoever they were. Fortunately for Jason, it was as if the *Dictionary of Forgotten Languages* had been made specifically to help him with this task. Using the information from the book, he managed to identify and separate the various words that composed the palindrome.

When the words had been divided and organized, the motto read like this:

es pet omemor suiba abius romemot epse

At that point the *Dictionary of Forgotten Languages* did miracles. In less than a quarter of an hour, Jason had all of the words translated into their modern equivalent. He proudly read the decoded message to his partners:

"*We move swiftly in the night, fearing the blazing fire.*"

"Well?" Julia said. "Does that mean anything to anybody?"

There was a long moment of silence. Finally, Rick spoke up. "I know which door will take us below." He walked up to the door through which they had entered. The door on which the albatrosses were engraved.

"As I said before, these are migratory birds. At night, they sleep on the waves, on rocks, or in haarbours. Which means we can eliminate them – since they don't move swiftly in the night."

He walked over to the door with the fish. He dismissed it with a wave, commenting, "Fish don't worry about fire. Enough said."

He stood before the door with the herd of bulls. Rick said, "But these animals might move around at night. And they might be afraid of a blazing fire. Hunters in ancient times used fire to hunt them, driving entire herds off cliffs."

"What a way to go," Julia said.

"But," Rick continued, "I don't think the motto refers to them. I don't think they were particularly swift at night. It doesn't fit."

Finally, Rick walked up to the final archway, which opened up into an impenetrable darkness. He raised his candle to light up the shape of the three moths that were carved into the stone.

"The motto is talking about these moths," he concluded with absolutely certainty. "They move swiftly at night and they are afraid of blazing fires, because fire attracts them – and destroys them."

Julia could now make out what appeared to be the shape of a skull carved on the back of one of the moths. "But if this is the right doorway," she asked, "why is there a skull carved on that moth? A skull to me means death."

Rick disagreed. "That's not a skull. It is just a spot

on its body, which might look like skull, but it's only an illusion."

"You sound pretty sure of yourself," Jason said.

Rick continued staring at the engraving. "That's because I am," he stated. "This is the way."

Jason reached his arm out, pushing the candle towards the dark passage, hoping to glimpse something of the path ahead. He said, "The message said *Of four three the motto will show.* There are three moths engraved in this archway." He looked at Julia. "Rick's right. This is the way to go."

Rick paused. "Remember, guys. We don't necessarily have to do it now."

"Oh, please," Julia said, playfully pushing him out of the way. "We didn't come this far just to give up. Let's see this through to the end."

Despite Julia's bravado, Jason took the lead. He lowered his candle to get a better view of the passageway. There was a flight of steep steps that led down below.

"This is it!" he cried. "There are stairs going down, just like the message says!"

Rick and Julia followed him cautiously. The steps were carved into solid rock, as were the walls that surrounded them. The further down they went, the more they could smell the pungent odour of the sea, which was carried up by little gusts of air. The walls were covered with a damp, glistening layer of brine.

Jason kept pushing onwards, leading the way, not looking back. He was about five steps ahead of the others. His candle cast glimmering reflections on the stairway's rough stone walls.

Little by little, the darkness became deeper and deeper and the light from their candles seemed dimmer and dimmer.

"Jason," Julia called, suddenly nervous. The draughts of air were becoming more and more insistent. Something felt wrong. "I'm not sure about this. Maybe we should go back up? Work things out."

Jason didn't reply. He only pushed onwards.

Moments later, he called out, "Rick, Julia! Come and see this!"

Julia instinctively grabbed Rick's arm. They made the rest of the way down hand in hand.

The stairway had come to an end. The ceiling of the passageway was only slightly higher than their heads and sloped down even further.

A few metres ahead of them, Jason had bent over to move aside some rocks that were blocking the little tunnel. The rocks let in streams of cold air, which whirled up along the stairway.

"Jason," Julia said. Fear was grabbing hold of her.

Her brother motioned for Julia to be silent. He moved the last rock and raised one finger towards his ear, gesturing for them to listen.

And now they heard it. It was distant and muffled, yet unmistakable. It was the sound of the sea.

"The grotto," Rick whispered.

"We're getting close," Jason said. "It sounds like it's right on the other side of these walls."

Julia looked into the narrowing, black tunnel. It didn't seem safe. "What if we've made a mistake?" she asked. "What if we've come through the wrong door?"

Jason ignored her fears. He got down on all fours and used his candle to light the tunnel. Every instinct in his body told him the same thing: "Go. Explore. Lead the way."

He crawled through the opening.

Rick and Julia heard him panting, struggling. Then, moments later, Jason exulted, "I did it! I'm standing up, guys! Come on!"

"What do you see?" Rick asked. He motioned for Julia to go first. "I'll be right behind you," he said reassuringly.

Jason's voice carried through the tunnel, echoing eerily. "The passageway is taller now, and keeps going straight on, like before! And then, wait, I think it turns to the left."

Julia muttered unhappily as they climbed through the cramped tunnel. The rock was cold and damp beneath her fingers. It scraped her knees and hands. "I should be shopping," she grunted, "not crawling through tunnels like a mole."

But just as Jason had said, she soon came to an opening. She stood up, looking for her brother.

Rick emerged from the tunnel after her. She reached out a hand and helped him up. "I'm getting too old for this," he joked.

Julia laughed. Maybe there was hope for Rick yet. It was nice to see him loosen up a little. She brushed the hair from her face and noticed that her skin was cold. She held a candle to Rick's face. It was streaked with dirt and sweat. He clutched the *Dictionary of Forgotten Languages* in his hand.

He saw Julia's gaze fall on the book. "I'm not letting go of this," Rick said. He turned his head all around, trying to get his bearings. "We should have brought some torches," he commented.

"True," Julia said. "A ham sandwich wouldn't have been a bad idea, either."

They heard Jason's footsteps further ahead. "We'd better hurry if we want to catch up with our fearless leader," Rick said. He took Julia by the hand and they hurried to find Jason.

Finally reunited, the three children walked together in single file. First Jason, then Julia, then Rick. When the tunnel turned sharply to the left, they were struck by a *whoosh* of air that immediately blew out the candles. They were in the dark.

Thud.

The noise came from above, high above. Rick turned, listening hard. "Guys?" he said. "You know the door we came through to get here? Well, I think it just slammed shut."

A wave of fear rippled through Julia. Something clammy brushed against her arm and she let out a shriek.

"Hey, it's only me," Jason said. He held his sister firmly by the arms. "It's just me," he repeated.

"Let's stay calm, all of us," Rick said. They huddled close together. "We need to light the candles again."

Rick pulled out his lighter and tried to light the candles. But the cold draughts kept blowing them out. "It's impossible to do it here," he said at last. "We'll have to find a better spot that's protected from the wind."

"If we form a shield, then it'll work," Jason suggested.

"Forget it," Rick replied. "The wind will only blow the candles out again. We'll have to make do with the flicker from this lighter until we can reach a better spot."

"Let's go back," Julia said. "We can get torches, supplies. We're not really prepared for this."

"We can't go back," Jason replied. "I'm sorry, Julia. There's no other way. The door to Argo Manor is shut."

"I've got the keys," Rick said, patting his pocket.

"I'm not sure that will help," Jason replied. "Were there locks on this side of the door? I can't remember."

There was a long moment of silence, broken only by the howling of the wind and by the eerie, muffled sound of the sea crashing on rocks.

"I can't remember, either," Rick confessed. "But I could go back and check it out."

"No," Julia said. "Don't go, Rick. Let's stick

together." She touched his arm. With her other hand she touched Jason's arm. "All of us." She took a deep breath. "I'm better now," she said apologetically. "It was just a stupid case of nerves. Let's work this thing out."

Using the flickering lighter to show the way, they began to explore their surroundings a little more closely.

"That was weird," Rick said. "When we turned, there was a sort of sudden blast of wind. Almost as if when we moved those rocks, we created an air stream leading up to Argo Manor. That's what made the door slam shut."

Jason considered it carefully. "The wind only started when we reached just here," he said. "It's like the air is coming from somewhere nearby. But where?"

Jason slowly inched forward. Beneath his toes he felt . . . nothing. The wind rose up from his feet into his face. "Oh no," he said with alarm. "Don't move another step, guys. There's a pit here. That's where the cold air is coming from."

It was true. Where there should have been a solid rock floor, there was none. Only emptiness.

"I get the feeling that someone doesn't want us here," Julia said.

"What do you mean?" Jason asked.

"The air current blew out our candles," Julia said. "We're trapped down here. In the dark. So we would fall down into that pit."

Rick quoted a line from the message: "*Of four two mean death on the spot.*"

"You and me, Julia," Jason said. "We almost fell down that pit together. That was really close."

"I'm not convinced," Rick said. "Think like scientists for a change. Air travels in currents. It moves to fill voids." He made a sweeping gesture with his arm. "The air current was pulled up. From upstairs."

"The window!" Jason said. "The window at the top of the tower might have opened again."

"Could be," Rick agreed. "Sure. The window created a draught between the round room and the stairway. You opened up the passage. And now we're stuck down here next to this huge hole."

Jason drifted into thought. Then he spoke slowly, as if he were thinking out loud. "Do you guys think that if we got past this hole in the floor, we could light our candles again?"

"But how can we get past it?" Julia asked. "We don't know how deep it is, or how wide. We don't have anything to light the way, we don't have rope, and we don't even know what's on the other side."

Rick tried to keep his mouth shut, but found that he couldn't. "I told you we should have brought rope."

Julia punched him gently on the shoulder. "Next time, Rick, I promise to listen," she said. It was probably as close to an apology as Rick was going to get.

"We have to go back," Julia said decisively. "There's no other choice. Once we get there, we'll see if we can open the door from the inside."

"Sounds reasonable," Rick agreed. "It's like you said. What choice do we have?"

"Well," Julia mused. "Another option is we could stay here in this freezing tunnel, next to the Black Pit of Death, and die a slow, agonizing death by starvation."

"You're hungry, aren't you?" Rick joked.

"Famished," she replied. "I'd give anything for a chocolate bar."

Julia turned to Jason.

"Jason?" she said. Then louder, "Jason?"

He was gone.

- Chapter 17 -
JASON'S LEAP

Jason was only a few steps away, but he might as well have been on the other side of the world. That's how it was when he started thinking. It was a strange sensation, like wheels spinning, turning inwards. The outside world fell away from him. And Jason was alone – away from people, places, even time. Just Jason and his thoughts. He never told anyone about it, though he suspected that it wasn't normal. He secretly feared that one day his mind would start spinning away and he would never find his way back again.

That idea frightened him very much.

Now he stood at the edge of the pit. The cool air rose up, sliding across his face like a cold caress. It smelled of the sea.

He could hear the discussion between Julia and Rick. They talked of going back. Of rope and chocolate bars. And Jason knew they were wrong. He wanted to continue onward. They couldn't fail now. Besides, they had no choice. There would be no turning back. Jason wouldn't allow it.

Jason considered the word *pit*. It was a frightening word, describing a chasm that was bottomless, dark, and vast. An endless fall.

But they did not know for certain that this pit was like that. They had lost their candlelight just before they had realized what stood in front of them. If only that gust of wind hadn't started up. If only they had used some other kind of light instead of candles.

Wait. A different kind of light. Maybe they had one. Maybe it was with them all along, a gift from the cliff.

Jason clutched the wooden box in his hands. The box full of – could it be? – earth-lights.

When the grotto's darkness seems defeat,
these earth-lights you may use
to shine a light upon the fleet. . .

Jason opened the box. His hand reached in, almost involuntarily, and dropped a few clay balls into the black emptiness.

One, two, three. Jason listened intently. The balls bounced against something, shattered, their fragments continuing their descent.

Jason heard Julia calling him. But he could not answer her. His mind was elsewhere, travelling into the deep, listening to the sound of the little balls.

They are bouncing against something, Jason thought. He threw a few more out in front of him. A moment of stillness, *tock tock tock*, and then silence again. It couldn't be a bottomless pit. The little balls of earth were bouncing against rocks on the other side, and that didn't seem particularly far away.

He threw another one, a bit further.

A moment of stillness, *tock tock tock*, then silence.

A third throw, even further. One *tock*. The clay ball had stopped without falling. It had landed on the other side!

They weren't standing before a vast pit. It was just a crevice of some kind. A crack in the passageway, not deep at all. And perhaps not that wide.

But how wide? How far across? A metre? Five metres? Maybe less.

For a second, Jason glimpsed a tiny light, a feeble little point that glowed in the spot where he had thrown the clay ball.

It was a glimmer of light, a glimmer that had faded in an instant.

"How could that be?" he wondered. "Could it be real?"

"Jason! Jason!" Julia cried out.

She was just behind him, but a million miles away.

Jason exhaled the air from his lungs. When they were empty, he let the box of clay balls fall into the emptiness.

And he jumped.

*   *   *

It was, quite literally, a leap in the dark. A leap into empty space, into mystery, into the unknown.

For some reason that he could never understand, Jason did it with complete trust. Was that the word? Trust? Perhaps faith. It was a feeling that he'd be safe. His destiny was not to die in some dark tunnel. No, he was meant for something more. Jason felt sure of it.

His body sailed into the unknown while below him dozens of balls of earth-light plummeted downwards, swallowed by the darkness.

He jumped because he knew it was the right thing to do. Because he and Julia and Rick had taken the passage that led below. He jumped because there are times in life when you must find the courage to jump. Without assurances, without guarantees of a safe landing. Just jump.

The hero doesn't choose his path. He simply follows it to the end.

And so, Jason's leap came to an unexpected end.

He landed on solid stone.

He had reached the other side.

Rick and Julia had heard the noises the balls of clay made when they fell into the empty space. They had heard Jason's leap without understanding exactly what they were hearing.

Then they heard laughter. Happy, giddy laughter. Jason's laughter. It was a sound they were glad to hear.

"Guys! I did it!" Jason exclaimed. "It's not that far across. You can do it, too!"

"Jason? I don't understand," Julia called.

"I jumped over it!" he said.

"What do you mean, you jumped?" Julia cried. "It's pitch-black in here. We can't even see."

"I used the balls of earth from the box," Jason explained. "I threw them down into the hole. I heard that they bounced back and forth way too much. So I realized that the pit wasn't that deep. And I decided to risk it."

"You decided to risk it?" Julia said incredulously. "You decided to jump even though you couldn't see? Are you crazy, Jason?"

Jason didn't say anything. But he thought, *Maybe.*

How could he explain the sensations he'd felt? The isolation. The strange certainty. He could not say why he'd let the box of clay balls drop into the hole. Or why he now understood the reason they were called earth-lights.

Finally he spoke. "Well, sue me," he said. "I went ahead and did it. I'm not sorry."

Rick moved to the edge of the pit. He asked Jason if it was windy on his side.

"No, it's not bad," Jason answered.

"Perfect," Rick answered. He reached back for Julia's hand. "We'll jump together," he whispered. "You and me."

"You and me," she repeated.

One, two, three. They ran, leaped. . .

. . .and landed on the other side.

Rick quickly lit the candles. Now with light, they could see what they had just crossed. The pit looked as if it had been man-made. They saw the remains of some old rusty hinges embedded in the rock.

"Maybe there used to be a cover over that hole – a grate or something," Rick guessed.

"Let's go," Julia said gruffly. "Let's just keep on going."

They moved forward without talking for several minutes. Julia took the lead, walking briskly. Then the passageway came to a sudden end.

"What now?" Julia groaned. "We have to stop again! Does everything have to be such a pain in the. . ."

"Julia, it's not a dead end. We're in a room of some kind," Jason said.

Rick held up his candle and turned in a slow

circle. The floor was made of squared rocks similar to those in the room they had found just beyond the door. The ceiling was crossed by a thick stone ribbing, like in a Gothic cathedral. There seemed to be no way out other than the way they'd come in.

"It looks like a dead end," Rick said. "But looks can be deceptive."

Rather than give up in the face of this new obstacle, the three explorers began to search the walls, floor, and ceiling, holding out their candles in every direction.

"It's like we're being put to the test," Jason muttered.

"We can't pass GO or collect two hundred pounds until we work this out," Julia agreed.

"But who built this room?" Rick wondered. "Who's putting us to this test?"

Julia seemed more determined than ever. She was tired, worn out, hungry, and now, finally, angry. She stood in the room's centre and glowered.

"I can't find a way out," Rick said softly. He continued feeling around on the slightly curved walls. He noticed how the rock walls joined together with the rock ribbing in the ceiling, just like the planks joined with the keel of a boat.

A boat?

The more he thought about it, the more Rick had the impression that they were *inside* a boat that was turned upside-down! He remembered the days when he used to hide under the small fishing boats out on the beach. The old fishermen would flip them over to dry in the sun.

Rick traced the stone rib with his finger. He said to the others, "To me, it feels like we're inside an upside-down boat." He pointed out the keel of the ceiling and the tapering shape of the room. "Do you see it?"

Jason tilted his head doubtfully. "Not exactly, but let's say that you're right. How do we get out of an upside-down boat?"

"There isn't really much of a trick to it," Rick said with a shrug. "You just grab the bottom of one side and lift."

It was such a far-fetched idea, they all immediately agreed that it was worth a try. They felt the intersection between the floor and the walls, centimetre by centimetre.

"Stone, stone, stone," Rick complained.

From the middle of the room, Julia began to count. "One, two, three, four. . ."

After circling the room, Jason and Rick stopped

searching. "It's just rock all the way around," Jason said. "There's nothing to grab on to."

CLACK! went something heavy, running along the stone.

Jason and Rick were startled by the loud noise. They spun around to look at Julia. She was crouching in the centre of the room.

At her feet, something once again went *CLACK!*

And then again, *KER-KER-KER-CLACK!*

"Fear not, boys," she announced with satisfaction. "I believe that I've found something." Julia bowed her head. "That's OK, ladies and gentlemen, no need for applause."

Nestor walked to the window in the tower and pulled it shut.

"One of these days I'll fix this," he mumbled, looking around.

As soon as he closed the window, the icy draught that had been coming up from the stairs was cut off. Nestor took a long look at the fleet of model ships resting beside the table. He saw that the diary beneath *Nefertiti's Eye* had vanished. He walked out of the room and closed the mirrored door behind him.

In the darkness of the house, he saw the reflection of a man whose features were hidden in the shadows. There was a long moment of silence as he studied the figure.

"The three children went through the door," Nestor said softly.

The storm crashed against Argo Manor.

"Good. Just as I hoped they would," the shadowy man replied.

"The door was slammed shut."

"Oh? Was that wise?"

The old man looked around, uncertain of the answer, and began to leave. He resisted the temptation to race down the stairs. He turned again to face the familiar figure. "The children are wise," he said. "Very wise, and very lucky. But most of all, they are very good. Pure hearts, courage – and the one has a gift. He is different. They deserve a chance to try."

The voice responded in protest. "They have no explanations, no advice. They could have been hurt. They could still get hurt. They might not succeed. What then?"

"They are bright children," Nestor said. "And there is something special about the one."

There was a long pause.

"Is this not too much to ask of a boy, only eleven years on this earth?" the voice asked.

"He has been chosen. It was not an accident," Nestor answered.

The man shook his head. "No, it was random. Just luck."

Nestor did not reply. His hobbled gait took him down the stairs. He limped into the stone room and glanced at the wardrobe, which had been moved aside. He stared at the door, which was shut tight. Julia, Jason, and Rick had taken the four keys with them. Nestor grimaced, then went to the front porch of the house. He slid his hand softly against the base of the statue of the fisherwoman, then picked up his oilskin raincoat from the ground.

He opened the front door wide to greet the howling rain.

The words of a moment ago still echoed through his mind. He knew perfectly well that Jason, Julia, and Rick had been chosen at random. But there weren't choices. Not in this. It was either their destiny or the fate of Ms Oblivia Newton.

Nestor reached into his pocket. He turned a coin over in his hand, ruminating on it. "Chance," he said, flicking the coin into the air with his thumb. "Luck." He snatched at the coin, slapped it into his palm. Heads.

"Sometimes luck is all that remains. Fate's last little joke," he mumbled. Then he walked out into the rain.

In the centre of the room there were four large rocks positioned one beside the other. Julia had discovered that with a little pressure, each one of the four rocks could rotate ninety degrees.

"The solution must be with these rocks," Julia said. "Can't you hear the noise they make when I turn them?"

"I think you're right," Rick agreed. "But how should we turn them? And what will happen when we do?"

Julia wasn't interested in another prolonged and agonizingly dull discussion. She simply began moving the four stones.

"Are you sure you should be doing that, Julia?" her brother asked.

"Am I sure?" Julia echoed. "Of course not." She continued rotating the rocks. "I'm sick and tired of talking about everything. Let's just *do* something for a change."

With the last turn of a rock, the room rumbled. It felt to Jason like an underground vibration.

"Something's happening," Jason warned.

The children braced themselves and waited. But the rumbling faded and disappeared. Julia once again began to push and pull on the four stones in the floor.

"*One of four will lead below*, isn't that right?" she asked Rick and Jason. "Well, then, come on, stones! Lead below!"

Clank, clank, clank.

The floor trembled. They heard a metallic noise, like that of a weight running along ancient cogwheels.

"I think it's working," Julia said. She stood up.

With a sudden *thud*, the furthest stone on the right opened up.

"A trapdoor!" exclaimed Jason. It was true. The stone moved to reveal a small opening in the floor.

"How in the world did you manage that?" Rick asked. He looked at Julia with genuine astonishment.

The candles were burning down to dangerous levels. To conserve them, Rick, Jason, and Julia decided to keep only one lit at a time. The light grew dimmer and they strained to see into the hole.

"What is it?" Rick wondered. "Another stairway?"

He reached a hand down and groped around in the darkness, while Jason held the stubby candle down as far into the hole as he could.

"It's smooth," Rick reported. "It's wet, slippery. It feels like a waterslide you'd find at an amusement park. I think it's a chute of some kind! Weird."

The children sat down on the floor, not sure how to proceed. They stared at the opening of the chute, which was just big enough for one of them to crawl through. If they wanted to find out where it led, only one could go at a time.

"If only we'd brought rope," Rick complained for what seemed to Julia to be the millionth time.

"Oh, stop moaning about the rope," she said, rolling her eyes.

Rick glared at her, puzzled and insulted. "Why are you getting on my case?"

"Hey, let's all calm down," Jason said. "It's been a long journey. We've been through a lot to get this far. Let's keep our cool."

"I've got an idea!" Julia exclaimed. She went to pick up the dictionary, weighing it in her hands. "Check this out." And with that, she knelt beside the trapdoor and dropped the dictionary down the chute. It silently vanished into the darkness.

Rick stared at Julia in stunned disbelief.

Julia ignored him. She leaned over to listen. All she heard was the dictionary sliding, sliding, sliding. Until she could hear it no longer.

"Are you crazy?!" Rick said angrily. "Would you mind telling me what you were thinking? You just threw away the one really useful thing we had left!"

Julia scratched her head, unfazed. "I don't know. I didn't really think about it all that much. I figured maybe we'd hear something, like if it fell into water or something."

Rick raised his hands in frustration. "And what if it did fall into water?"

Julia could see that he was getting upset. "Well," she reasoned, "we would have learned that the chute led to water."

"Oh great," Rick muttered. "And we would have ended up with a ruined dictionary."

"Well, it's gone now," Jason said.

"Yes, it is gone now!" Rick shouted. "Don't you two get it? This is serious. And both of you keep doing stuff without thinking." He pointed an accusing finger at Jason. "You leap before you look. Like, wow, here's a huge hole in the ground – I think I'll jump over it!" Then he turned to Julia. "And you're even worse. What were you thinking? Did you ask yourself, 'Hmmmm, what really valuable thing can I flush down this hole?'"

Rick waved his arms in anger and frustration. "You two don't even take a second to think. You just . . . *do* stuff. *Aaaarrrggghhh!*" He spun around and stamped off, grumbling to himself.

Jason and Julia looked at each other, surprised by Rick's reaction.

"Well, wasn't that special?" Julia said. It was a joke, but it didn't feel funny.

"He's angry," Jason whispered.

"No, you think so?" Julia replied in mock surprise.

Still, she knew that Rick had a point. Maybe she should have thought about it a little more. Maybe throwing that dictionary down the chute wasn't the brightest thing in the history of womankind. But, she reasoned, so what? She was the one who'd opened the trapdoor. Sometimes you just have to act. She glanced at Rick, who was on the other side of the room, scowling. A knot formed in her stomach.

"I'll talk to him," Jason said.

Julia sat down and sighed. She let her feet dangle off the edge of the chute, disappearing into the black. She stretched the soles of her trainers until they touched the chute's smooth sides. She was discouraged. But she knew she had to make things right.

"The dictionary survived," she whispered to herself. "So can I."

She slowly lowered her body down. "Guys," she called out. "I'll see you later." And she let herself drop into the chute, into the unknown, into mystery.

"Julia, no!" Rick cried.

But she was already gone.

Jason and Rick ran to the edge of the trapdoor,

straining to hear. A cry came up. "YEEEEE-HOOOOO!" Julia yelled from somewhere far below. And then – nothing.

"Julia!" Jason yelled into the hole. "Julia! JULIAAAAA!"

Rick put his hand on Jason's shoulder as if to silence him. "Shhh," he whispered.

Then from very far away, they heard Julia's voice. "I'm OK," she called. "It's incredible! It's fantastic! Guys! You have to see this."

A huge smile broke across Jason's face. "She's OK!"

Rick nodded happily, beaming back at Jason.

Laughing, too impatient to wait another moment, they, too, let themselves slip through the trapdoor.

Jason slid on his back at a dizzying speed, jiggling from time to time along the smooth stone. The chute was moist, slippery, and as fast as an Olympic bobsleigh course.

After an initial moment of pure terror, he felt an uplifting sensation. Just as Julia had before him, Jason opened his mouth to let out a gleeful scream at the first hairpin turn. It certainly helped to distract him from the terrifying fact that he was hurtling at dangerous speeds to points unknown.

The further Jason travelled, the less the chute sloped, although he continued to slide along like a bullet in a chamber. At the end, he was catapulted on to a sandy beach.

Jason rolled over and opened his eyes wide, realizing at that moment that he'd kept them shut the entire journey. The first thing he saw, right in front of him, was the *Dictionary of Forgotten Languages*.

Then he saw Julia, smiling, happy. And – the grotto. They had made it.

Julia gestured with her arm. "Look at this place, Jason. It's amazing."

Gentle waves of seawater lapped against the sandy beach. Jason looked all around. The grotto was closed in by gigantic walls of rock. High above them danced hundreds of tiny flashing lights. Other lights were blinking, one by one, along the inner walls of the cavern.

Jason rose to his feet. "Earth-lights," he murmured, as he watched the little points of dancing light.

"No," Julia said, facing him. She was holding one of the little balls of clay, which she carefully broke open. Inside was the trembling little body of an insect. "It's a firefly, Jason," she told him.

"Fireflies," the boy said in wonder.

"Ooooooof!" cried a voice behind them.

Rick tumbled on to the beach, planting his face in the sand.

"Oh. Look who dropped in," Julia deadpanned.

Jason, Julia, and Rick stood at the edge of the beach, looking around at the grotto in awe. All around them flickered hundreds of fireflies, giving off a soft glow like the light that comes right before dawn on a summer's day. The ceiling was dark and seemingly as distant as the night sky. The walls sank down into the sea pool, which formed a mirror of water that moved gently. The sound of waves came from outside, on the other side of the grotto walls, where the open sea thundered against the rocks.

The white beach was small, just a spit of sand, large enough for only a dozen people to fit comfortably. A short wooden pier stretched out into the sea pool.

Where a great ship was moored.

Jason, Julia, and Rick gaped at it in disbelief.

The ship was intimidating, a craft with a massive body, a tall bow and stern. A long row of oars was raised up, as if standing at attention, at the two sides of the ship. The keel bobbed up and down with the movements of the sea, causing a slight jangling of a chain that dropped down into the water.

Rick drank in every detail of the mighty craft. He felt as if he were in the presence of something holy, like an altar at church. "Wow!" was all he could murmur.

"This must have belonged to old Ulysses Moore," Jason said.

"It looks like a Viking ship," Rick said. "At least, I think it does."

Julia again searched the grotto with her eyes. "I don't understand," she said. "There's no way out of here."

She was right. There was no exit to the sea, no way out of the massive cave. The grotto contained a sea pool, and in that pool was the enormous ship. "It's just like the ship in the bottle at Argo Manor," Julia remarked. "How did it get here? And where do you think we are, exactly? Is this the grotto of the ancient druids?"

"I guess they built the ship inside here," Rick speculated. "Maybe it was made by the same people who built the passageway."

"Okaaay," Julia said. "Why?"

"Why?" Rick repeated.

"Yeah, why build a ship inside a cave?" Julia asked. "It doesn't exactly make a lot of sense."

Jason stared at the grotto's ceiling. "We must be inside the cliff underneath our house," he said. "Does that sound right to you, Rick?"

Rick nodded in agreement. It made no logical sense – a boat inside a cave inside a cliff. But Rick was learning that when it came to Argo Manor, maybe he needed to let go of logical thinking. Like Jason's leap of faith across the pit, or Julia's fall into the chute, Rick had to let go of ordinary logic and embrace . . . the magical.

That's what this was, wasn't it? Pure magic, the purest kind of wonder on this earth. A ship in a bottle!

Jason whistled. "I'd say this place hasn't been visited for a long, long time."

"How do you know that?" Julia asked.

"Didn't you notice the awful state of the passageway?" he asked. "Rocks had crumbled in the way, everything had fallen into disrepair. It's like a pathway forgotten by time."

"What about these fireflies?" Julia asked. "How come nobody in Kilmore Cove ever saw light shining through a few cracks? How come they never noticed that the cliff lit up at night?"

Rick didn't answer immediately. "Maybe they did notice," he said at last. "Some people, I mean. But even if you saw faint light coming from the cliff at night – who could have imagined this?"

"Well, what do you think?" Jason asked.

Rick shook his head. "No one would work it out. It could have been a reflection from the lights in the houses. Or the lighthouse reflecting off the rocks on the shore, reflecting back against the cliff. Who knows?"

Julia eyed Rick carefully. "Maybe your father knew something," she guessed. "He was a fisherman, wasn't he?"

Rick shook his head. "My father never told me anything about a ship like this," he said. "He never said anything about this place. My father had nothing to do with Argo Manor."

"So there's no way this ship ever left the grotto?" Jason asked.

Rick made a face. "Left? How could it? There's no way out! Besides, suppose there is a magical way of – I don't know – opening the wall. Somebody in town would have seen something. There'd be stories, tall tales about a Viking ship. But there's nothing."

"But didn't you say before that Ulysses Moore once owned a ship?" Julia prodded.

"Not like this," Rick said. He began to walk up the pier towards the ship. The old boards creaked beneath his feet. Jason and Julia cautiously followed him. They looked at the empty oar-pegs on the side. They stared at the long oars that were raised upwards, on end, like a line of soldiers at attention. Julia became absorbed by the mainmast, which was four times taller than the oars and as solid as an oak tree.

It swayed gracefully, ever so slightly, back and forth.

Rick walked up to the bow, a majestic curve of carved wood. "She is perfect, don't you think?" he said, caressing the wood. "I mean, if I had to draw a perfect ship, I'd make her just like this. With this same shape, the same mainmast, the oars, just like ships from ancient times."

"Does it have a name?" Jason asked.

"That's what I'm trying to find out," Rick replied.

On the keel was engraved:

ΜΕΤΙΣ

"*Metie,*" Rick read.

"Excuse me?"

"*Metie,*" Rick repeated. "This ship is called the *Metie.*"

"What a bizarre name," Julia said.

"I'm not sure how to pronounce it correctly," Rick said. "The last letter isn't really an *e.* I doubt this word is in English."

"You're not wrong there," Julia said. "It's not like any word I've ever seen." She ran back to shore to pick up the dictionary. Carefully brushing it off, she showed it to Rick. "Safe and sound," she said.

"And not the least bit wet," Rick noted with a wink.

"How about we climb on board?" Jason suggested.

Rick grabbed a long board, a gangplank, and placed it between the pier and the ship. He was about to step on board, but then he thought better of it. He stepped aside, bowed and gestured to Jason.

"After you, Captain Jason Covenant," Rick said.

"Very well," Jason replied in a haughty tone. "Tonight we'll be dining on the main deck."

And with that, he boarded the ship, followed closely by his first mates, Rick Banner and Julia Covenant.

The ship had a single deck, which hid the hold in the ship's belly. On either side of the craft was a row of ten wooden benches, each one lined with oars that stood upright. Each oar was chained to an oar-peg.

"They chain the oars to keep from losing them in rough water," Rick explained.

"*Metis!*" Julia exclaimed. She read hastily in the

dictionary, then explained, "That last letter is like an *s*. It's a word from ancient Greek."

"Does it mean anything?" Rick asked.

"Hmmm, let's see," Julia said, running her finger down the page. "*Metis* means wisdom. It was the name of Zeus' first wife, who was the daughter of Oceanus and Thetis. Supposedly an intelligent, capable woman." Julia looked at Rick. "Like all women, of course!"

"Present company excluded," he teased.

"You'd better watch yourself, pal," Julia shot back.

She shut the dictionary and peered inside the hold. "It's empty," she said, clearly disappointed. "There's nothing in there at all."

Deep down, Julia hadn't completely given up the idea that they would find treasure at the end of their journey. A big ship was nice. It was amazing. But it wasn't quite the secret treasure she'd been imagining.

The ship was an empty shell. The mainmast, rising straight up from the centre of the deck, was without sails. There were only four thick ropes, covered with a layer of salt.

"No sails," Rick said quietly. "This ship has never been to sea – or at least not for a long, long time. But it seems sound and sturdy. It doesn't look like it's been attacked by teredines."

"Terror-whats?" Julia asked.

"Teredines," Rick repeated. "Shipworms that feed off wood."

"Like termites?" Julia said.

"Exactly," Rick answered. "They dig down into the boards and make nests. Bit by bit, they destroy the wood."

They walked to the back of the ship, called the stern. At the two sides of the hull, standing up on end, were two oars that were broader and flatter than the others. "These function as rudders," Rick explained, "for steering. You drop them down over the sides and manoeuvre them like this." He showed Jason how each of the two rudders had a crossbar sticking out, which gave them an *l* shape.

Jason found it all fascinating. "And what's that?" he asked Rick, pointing to a tiny wooden house at the stern, just behind the two rudders.

"I'd say that's the stateroom," Rick answered, walking towards its entrance.

Over the threshold of the cabin, there was an old tattered curtain decayed by salt air and time. Rick gently slid it aside and looked inside. It was dark, so he lit the stub of a candle.

The stateroom was almost completely bare. What remained of its old curtains hung in rags from the ceiling and walls, giving the space a haunted appearance.

On one side of the room there was a bed lodged between two old trunks. On the opposite side was a board bolted to the walls, which must have been used as a table. Lying on top was a candelabrum with three candles. Beside the candelabrum was a closed book.

Rick lit the three candles and touched the book.

"That could be the last captain's diary," Julia whispered from behind him.

Rick turned the black leather cover and opened the book.

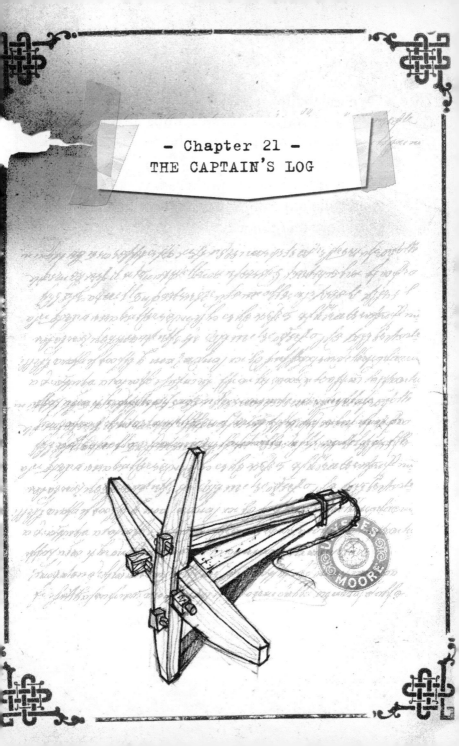

On the first page, in elegant handwriting, were these words:

17 September of the last year

This is likely to be the last journey of the Metis. Now, after having fulfilled our desires and taken us wherever we wished to go, she no longer has reason to set sail. The hands that guided the rudders can do so no longer. Mine have become too old for the task. Those of the person who once accompanied me are long gone. Time, that merciless ravager of flesh and blood, has brought our adventure to an end. Now that the anchor is resting at the bottom of this secret sea, all that is left to me are the memories of what we have seen and experienced, of what we have been through and learned. Also remaining with me are the dreams of the ports that I have not yet seen. I feel old now. And old, too, is our ship, although she's still capable of crossing all barriers of time by following the course charted by her captain's desires.

Now, my dear old ship, I desire that we come to a halt.

You, my ship, who were carved out of the wood from the sacred oak tree, I beseech you: lay your oars to rest! Your captain is finished, there is no one to command you. Rest easy. No longer do you have a Lady of the Thieves against whom to battle in the storm-swept wind.

May the night smile gently upon you, my beloved Metis, *because it is to the night I now entrust you.*

Rick, who had been reading aloud, paused for a moment. Jason and Julia hung on each word in silence.

"That's all there is," Rick said. He turned a few pages to reveal that the rest of the diary was empty.

"What do you think?" he asked.

"That was beautiful," Julia whispered, genuinely touched.

"I recognize the writing." Jason pulled out the diary they had found in the tower room. He placed it beside the captain's log and compared the handwriting. The letters were identical in shape and size. The two books had been written by the same hand.

"This is the last entry written by Ulysses Moore,"

Jason said. "It was his farewell message. It's almost as if he were writing to the ship itself."

"Herself," Rick corrected. "It's an old tradition. Sailors think of ships as being female."

"He talks about adventures, journeys, and distant ports," Julia said. "He must have done incredible things in this ship."

"Or more correctly, he *imagined* some incredible things," Rick said. "How could he have sailed this ship into the open sea?"

Jason flipped through the Egyptian diary, the one they had found in the tower. "But here," he said excitedly, "Ulysses talks about Egypt as though he had actually been there."

"Not in this boat!" Rick protested. "It doesn't have a motor, a boiler room, or even a sail! It's a beautiful boat, but no way could it sail to north Africa."

"It could be rowed, though!" Jason said.

Rick laughed. "Jason, can you imagine trying to find twenty people willing to row all the way from England to Egypt? I don't think so. And if he had, we would've heard all about it on TV!"

Jason looked acutely disappointed.

"Hey, look," Rick said. "This has been an amazing day. Maybe the greatest, coolest adventure of my life. We found this amazing ship. We learned that Ulysses Moore was a great writer with an incredible imagination. OK, maybe he was a little bit crazy, too. But so what? He could make fantastic adventures seem real."

"I suppose you're right," Jason reluctantly said. "But I can't help feeling there must be something more. . ."

Julia turned to Rick. "So what do we do now?" she asked.

"We go home," Rick replied. He walked out on to the deck and gazed up at the countless fireflies.

"Rick?"

Jason and Julia stared at him from the doorway to the stateroom. Rick turned and smiled. He said, "How do you guys reckon we get out of this cave?"

Out on deck, they had a better view of the entire grotto. The beach where the ship was moored had no visible exit, apart from the chute. The sea pool around them occupied the rest of the cave, with the exception of another tiny stretch of beach on the opposite side of the grotto. This second beach looked just like the one they'd come from. It, too, had a small wooden pier. But instead of a chute, the other beach had a narrow set of black steps that led up to a door. Above the door was a stone archway.

"Something tells me that we have to get to those steps," Julia said, "and go through that door."

"How do we get there?" Jason wondered. "Swim?"

Rick leaned over the ship's rail and looked down at the water. It was dark and forbidding. He judged the distance from one beach to the other, then shook his head. "That's a long, dangerous swim," he warned. "There could be underwater currents or whirlpools. Swimming wouldn't be my first choice."

They searched for some other way across. There was no bridge, no ridge along the cave wall to climb. Nothing connected the two shores.

Except, of course, for the sea.

Julia walked along the deck, thinking. "We could use the ship," she said. "Or is that just crazy?"

"What?" sputtered Rick. "Yes, it's crazy. It's crackers. It's bananas. Do you know how difficult it would be to move a ship like this? Who's going to work the oars? Who's going to steer the rudders?"

"Oh, Rick," Julia said, not unkindly. "You've got to lighten up. I thought it might be fun to try."

"And what about the anchor?!" Rick continued. "Would you care to pull it up, Julia?"

"OK, Rick. There's no need to be so uptight," Julia answered. Now she was the one getting annoyed.

Rick heard it in her voice. "I'm sorry," he apologized. "It's just that I've been around boats my entire life. My father died on a ship. He went off one day and never came back."

"I'm sorry," Jason said.

"A ship isn't a toy," Rick said softly. "You don't fool around with this stuff. You need knowledge, skill and strength."

Julia walked up to Rick and put a hand on his arm. "You're right," she said. "It was a stupid idea. I'm sorry, too."

Jason heaved a deep sigh. "Maybe not so stupid after all," he said. "We don't have many choices."

Rick looked at him questioningly.

"You don't give yourself enough credit, Rick," Jason said. "You've got knowledge, skill and strength. You know the sea. And you know how to do a lot of other things. How many hours have we been walking around in the dark on our own? Without you, we would never have made it this far."

Jason looked from Rick to his sister and back again. He had their full attention now, he could feel it. "We wanted to see this thing through to the end," he continued. "And we did it. We racked our brains to solve one riddle after the other. Crazy writings, hidden messages, trick locks – that's what I call skill. Oh, fine, you say it takes strength. And alone, we're not that strong. I'm not, that's for sure. We're just children. But together, we can do anything."

Julia and Rick hung on every one of Jason's words. They were ready to try anything. They just needed someone to lead them. Jason stood before Rick and put out his hand. "If you would tell us what to do and how to do it, we would give it everything we've got. Here we are, in this amazing grotto, on a ship that seems magical, and it all feels like destiny. Rick, I know this is what we're meant to do."

A slow grin swept across Rick's face. He grabbed Jason's hand and shook on it. "Let's do it," he said.

"Yes!" Julia exclaimed. "Awesome, awesome, awesome." She leaped up and hugged Jason and Rick. "We're going on a boat ride!"

Rick and Jason looked at the far shore. "I'd rather float in a boat than try swimming in that water," Jason whispered in Rick's ear. "What have we got to lose?"

Rick nodded. He was willing to give it a try.

"Let's get started," Jason said.

"Aye, aye, Captain Jason," Rick answered, giving Jason the sailor's salute. "Maybe this old girl has one more voyage left in her!"

- Chapter 22 -
ON TO THE PORTS OF DREAMS

Julia gathered everything that might come in handy. Her task was to take a quick inventory and place everything inside the stateroom.

Rick climbed the mainmast, using the small notches that were cut into it for that purpose. His job was to detach at least one of the four ropes that hung from the top. One way or another, Rick Banner was determined to get a rope.

He slowly began his climb. When he'd got about halfway up, Julia staggered out from the stateroom, laughing.

"Hey, Rick!" she cried. "Look at all the ropes! The trunks are full of ropes!"

Rick made a face. But he had to laugh. At last they'd found the one thing he thought they'd needed all along.

"So now that we've got the ropes," Julia said, "what do you want to do with them?"

Rick was all business. He checked their weight. Most of them, he noted, were hawsers, the kind typically used for mooring a ship. Some ropes were rotten and frayed, yet others were in remarkably good condition. Rick carefully laid them out on the deck. Then he led the twins to the capstan, which was used to raise the anchor. It still seemed to be in working order. The capstan was a wooden cylinder which, when rotated with a long, *L*-shaped handle, would pull the heavy chain up out of the water.

But when Rick gave it a push, the handle would not budge. It had rusted over time. Jason joined Rick, and they pushed shoulder to shoulder.

"Push!"

"Push!"

Julia went around to the other side. She pulled hard. "Put some muscle into it, you guys!" she hollered.

That was enough for the two boys. Just when they were about to give up, the handle let out a screech and began to move. With great effort, they managed to make a quarter-turn, then a half-turn, then finally a full turn.

A portion of the dripping chain wound around the cylinder. Slowly, the three sailors managed to hoist the heavy anchor. While Rick and Jason continued to work the capstan, Julia leaned over the side of the ship to check on their progress.

"I can see it!" she cried out at last. "We've done it!"

Now unanchored and unmoored, the ship began to drift ever so slightly on the surface of the enclosed sea.

Rick backed away from the capstan. He bent over,

hands on his knees, trying to catch his breath. "Jason," he said, "go to the rudders. Julia, lower a pair of oars, one starboard and one port-side!"

Julia looked at him blankly.

Rick smiled. "One on that side, one on the other," he said, pointing.

"Gotcha!"

Jason reached one of the two broad rudder-oars. He grabbed it by the handle and looked to Rick for guidance.

"Lower it!" Rick called out.

Jason plunked it down. The flat oar splashed into the water. Jason lost his balance and almost fell in along with it.

"Not like that! You have to keep it up against the ship!" Rick told Jason. "Hold it steady!"

Jason's eyes opened wide. "Easy for you to say," he protested.

"We're moving!" Julia called out, thrilled. "Wait, no, we aren't! Um, hold on. Yes, we are! We're moving in a circle!"

Rick shook his head. "You haven't spent much time on ships, have you?"

"I saw *Titanic*," she confirmed. "But actual time on an actual ship? Um, no. This would be my first time ever. But I love it!"

Julia was right about the ship. After the initial movement forward, the ship had stabilized in a repeated movement, as if it had met a circular current of water. It was moving slightly all the time, but going nowhere fast.

Rick lowered the oar on his side and called to Jason. "Jason, come here! This connecting rod will let you control both of the rudders. Hold it like this. Julia and I will work the oars. Just keep the rudders straight, OK? Make sure that the bow of the ship is aimed towards the door on the other side."

Jason nodded. He was determined to succeed.

Rick moved quickly towards Julia. He showed her how to grab the oar. "Do you know how to row?" he asked.

"I can learn," Julia replied.

Rick looked over his shoulder, desperate. This wasn't going to work. If they didn't start to row immediately, there was a risk that they might run the ship aground on the beach behind them. If that happened, it was all over.

"Change places with Jason," he ordered. "Quickly!"

Jason quickly slipped out of the way as Julia came to replace him. He hustled over to grab an oar.

"You know how to row, right?" Rick snapped.

"Of course!" Jason lied. He was thinking, *Hey, how hard could it be? You just pull. Or push. Or whatever.*

Rick nodded. "On three, we'll make the first stroke. Oar down, stroke, hoist, oar down, stroke, hoist. You got that?"

Jason nodded. He hadn't understood a word.

"One, two, three!" Rick shouted. He lowered his oar into the water, leaned into the heavy oar with the full weight of his body, and pushed. Then he raised it up again.

Jason tried to mimic Rick's motions. He heard the oar splash down into the water, pushed it painfully through the water, and then raised it up. So far, so good.

"Again!" Rick commanded. "And again!"

Jason threw all of his might into it. The effort was enormous and exhausting. After just a few hard pulls, his muscles strained and sweat formed on his back, drenching his shirt.

The ship did not move.

"Something's holding it in place!" Julia called out. "We're not moving!"

"No!" Rick blurted out. "It can't be!"

But the ship had not moved at all, not even in the

wrong direction. It was as if something invisible was holding the ship in place.

The children decided to take a break. Julia and Rick sat alone on the deck, each of them deep in their own private thoughts. Jason paced anxiously. He was beyond the point of exhaustion. Now his energy buzzed on overdrive.

A strange thought entered his mind. It was strange in that it didn't feel to Jason like he'd "thought" it. No, it was more like the idea came to him without any thought at all. And in truth, Jason's first reaction to it was: *ridiculous.*

He brushed the thought aside. But it persisted in nagging at him, like a dog nipping at his heels. Maybe there wasn't anything holding the ship in place. Maybe the *Metis* was ready to go. Maybe it was ready and . . . *waiting.*

The ship was here, waiting for them.

But something was missing: the destination. The reason for their journey. Maybe there was an instrument on board that was used to set the course, a guidance system of some kind.

Maybe the ship had some sort of revolutionary engine hidden in the hold, even if the hold looked absolutely empty.

It was crazy. Jason knew these thoughts were crazy. He couldn't explain or defend them. A logical, reasonable person like Rick wouldn't give them the time of day.

And yet. . .

Jason sensed that the ship itself was waiting to know where they wanted to go. Because it was a magic ship. In the captain's log, it said that the craft had been made from the wood of a sacred tree. Which meant that the ship, in some way, was sacred, too.

But sacred to whom?

Jason walked up to the rudder and grabbed it absently. But the ship didn't move.

"What are you doing, Jason?" Julia called out.

"Just fooling around," he answered.

Jason tried to relax. He let his thoughts flow through him. He tried *not* to think. In his mind's eye, he saw himself heroically guiding the ship through a storm, towards unknown lands. He saw the walls of the grotto open to reveal the vast sea. He saw the ship with full sails billowing in the wind, as if they had unfurled on their own.

"Are you ready to try rowing again?" Rick asked.

Jason shook his head. "No. It's not about rowing. That won't solve the problem," he replied slowly.

"I take it you have a better idea," Rick replied. "I'm all ears. How does she move? With sails? With an engine? Or in your dreams?"

Could it be? Could that be the answer? Jason thought about the words in the captain's log. What were they exactly?

Jason closed his eyes and remembered:

Now, after having fulfilled our desires and taking us wherever we wished to go. . .

He repeated the phrase aloud. "Wherever we wished to go."

Egypt!

Old Ulysses had visited there. He had been aboard this very ship. Jason was certain of it. He pulled out the tower diary that spoke of Egypt. It had rested beneath the lead ship in the fleet, *Nefertiti's Eye.*

His hand on the rudder, Jason whispered the word, "Egypt."

At that moment, he felt the rudder tremble between his fingers. Almost in answer to his wish.

A breeze scattered the fireflies. They began to fly in a spiral. "What's happening?" Rick asked, alarmed. "Where is the wind coming from?"

"Egypt," Jason said, more loudly this time.

Once again, the rudder vibrated in his hands. A

violent gust of air swept the fireflies away. The insects flew towards the recesses of the walls as if seeking shelter.

"Jason!" Julia cried. "Something really weird is happening!"

Jason nodded, smiling. Something was happening. The ship was responding to him. They were communicating, Jason and his ship. He slipped the diary into his pocket and grabbed the rudder with both hands.

"Hold on tight!" he warned Rick and Julia. Then he cried out in a clear, strong voice, "Take us to Egypt!"

"Jason! What are you screaming about?" Julia shouted. "The wind – I can't hear you!"

A strong blast of air hit the ship, knocking Julia flat on the deck.

"Hold on!" Jason cried. "No matter what happens, hold on for your life!"

The wood of the rudder started to jerk around in his hands, tugging violently in every direction.

"To Egypt!" Jason commanded. "Take me to Nefertiti. Take me to the treasures of Tutankhamen!"

The wind whipped around them. The sea swelled and surged. The fireflies disappeared.

And the grotto fell into total darkness.

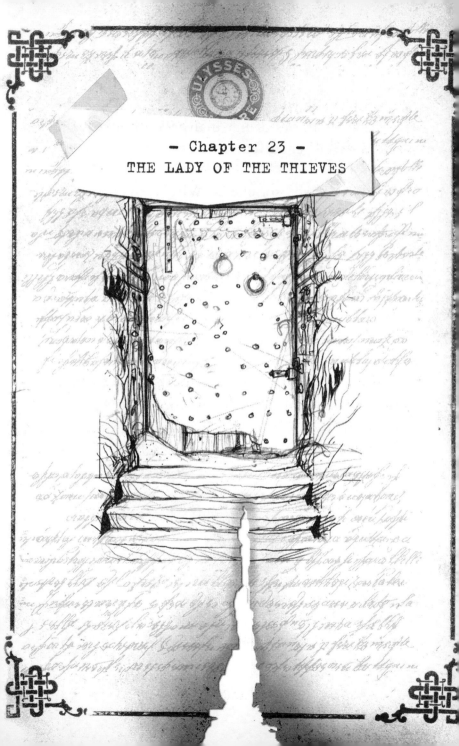

- Chapter 23 -
THE LADY OF THE THIEVES

Oblivia Newton walked briskly along the marble floors of her mansion. Manfred, the hatchet-faced chauffeur, rushed in through a side door.

"Manfred!" she shrieked. "Why are you pestering me?"

The young brute glared at her, his meaty knuckles white with hostility. "I'm sorry, Ms Newton," he said, lowering his head obediently. "I have something urgent to tell you."

Oblivia brushed past him indifferently. She had places to be.

Manfred hurried along behind her.

"I've been watching the three children," he said. "Just like you told me, Ms Newton."

Oblivia Newton stopped. She stood before a blue door, her hand on the knob. "The children," she sneered. "Are they enjoying themselves at Argo Manor?"

"They went down the cliff to take a swim," Manfred said.

Oblivia tapped her foot on the marble floor. "If there is a point to this story, Manfred," she said, bristling with annoyance, "please get there in a hurry."

"One of the boys fell when he was coming up the cliff," Manfred continued. "He caught hold of the cliff somehow. It looked like he found something in the rocks."

Oblivia's eyes narrowed. "Found something?"

"Yes, Ms Newton."

"Well, are you going to tell me what he found, you thickheaded mule?" barked Oblivia. "Or shall we play twenty questions?"

Manfred shrugged helplessly. "It was like a box or something," he said.

Oblivia nodded once, sharply. Her face remained expressionless.

"They rode their bikes into town," Manfred said. "They came back with some books."

"Charming. The little creatures read," Oblivia muttered. "Hopefully it will keep them busy and out of harm's way."

"Um, er, there's something else," Manfred stammered. He swallowed hard.

"What is it?" hissed Oblivia. "Don't just stand there clutching at your trousers. Spit it out."

"I think I saw a light glowing from the grotto," he said, wincing as he spoke the words.

Oblivia's face tightened in rage. "What?!" she screamed. "A light in the grotto? How could that be?"

Manfred shrugged unhappily. "I don't know, Ms Newton."

"Of course you don't know," she said darkly. "You are an ape in a monkey suit!"

She brought her thumb and middle finger to the bridge of her nose. "What is that old fool up to now?" she wondered aloud.

Oblivia fixed her gaze on Manfred. "We will continue as planned," she stated coldly. "Do you understand, Manfred? Nothing will stop me."

Manfred nodded obediently. "You can count on me, Ms Newton."

Oblivia turned her back to Manfred. But she paused before opening the door to the next room. "You did well, Manfred," she said.

She left through the door, closing it firmly behind her. Manfred stared at it hopelessly. "Thanks," he whispered, "Lady of the Thieves."

Back inside the grotto, the great ship pitched and rolled. It was trapped inside a fierce storm, blasted by wind and surging waves. Julia and Rick clung to the ropes, desperately hanging on for their lives.

Jason, however, seemed unaware of his surroundings. His eyes remained fixed, staring straight ahead. His hands gripped the rudder tightly.

"Almost there," he whispered to himself. "Almost there."

Just when it seemed like the ship was about to burst from the strain, the storm vanished.

Just that quickly. In a moment, it was gone. No waves, no wind. All was calm and still. The fireflies again swarmed high above them, as if nothing had happened.

Except for this.

The ship had settled at the far pier.

Jason sagged over the rudder, not noticing his surroundings. He was drained. Julia, drenched with cold water, stood on rubbery legs, shivering. Rick released the rope he had been holding and he examined the burn marks on his palms.

No one had the energy to utter a word. Everything that had just happened had been ovewhelming. Incomprehensible. Frightening, fantastic and surreal. The storm had not lasted more than two minutes. Yet they had been the most harrowing two minutes of the three children's lives.

Julia staggered towards her brother. "Jason," she called hoarsely.

Jason lifted his head and focused his eyes on his sister as if he were coming from a deep sleep. "What? What happened?" he asked.

Rick rubbed his torn, bleeding hands. He wearily

looked around at the ship's water-ravaged deck. He couldn't speak.

"We're on the other side," Julia told her twin.

Jason blinked. It was true: the ship was now sitting in tranquil waters on the far shore of the pool.

Jason allowed himself to smile. He hugged Julia with relief and together they pulled Rick into their embrace.

Julia pointed to the dark stairway, which led to a door.

Rick tugged uncomfortably at his wet clothes. A chill ran through his body. He noticed that Julia's lips were nearly blue. "We've got to get dry somehow," he said. "Get out of these clothes."

"There were clothes inside the trunk in the stateroom," Julia remembered.

The clothes in the trunk looked like they hadn't been worn in a long time. But they were dry and that was all that mattered. The children exchanged their wet clothes for ill-fitting trousers, loose shirts, and crude wooden sandals.

Julia looked at the two boys and frowned. "I am sooooo glad we don't have a mirror," she joked. "I don't want to even think about what I look like."

"You look nice," Rick said kindly. Ever the practical one, he couldn't care less about his appearance. He was simply grateful to be dry again, and warm. He gathered up their things – the dictionary, the journals, some candles – and led the others to dry land.

Worn and frazzled, still in a state of shock, they crossed the beach and climbed the black stairs.

"I'm fried," Julia confessed as they reached the door. "I need a nice long bath, some of Nestor's hot soup, and about three solid days of sleep."

"Four days for me," Rick commented.

Whatever thoughts were in Jason's mind – *Egypt?* he wondered – he kept to himself.

On the stone archway above the door was a carving of three turtles. Jason leaned against the door. To his surprise, it was not locked.

He turned to his friends, pausing with the doorknob in his hands. "Are you ready?" he asked.

Julia and Rick nodded.

Jason opened the door.

- Chapter 24 -
THE ADVENTURE BEGINS

Jason brushed the wet hair from his eyes. They had entered a well-lit corridor.

"It's hot," Rick commented. He felt the ground with his hand. "Sand," he said. "Hot sand."

Julia gazed at the blocks of stone that formed the walls around them. They were dark rock, totally different from those inside the grotto.

Rick felt an urge to return to the door they had just passed through. But when he glanced back, it had blended into the stone walls. If he had not known it was there, Rick would have sworn that the door had turned to stone.

"Careful, everyone," Jason warned. "Stick together."

They turned a corner and found themselves standing in another corridor with a steep, narrow staircase leading up. Bright light poured through a grate in the ceiling.

Julia squinted, her eyes adjusting to the brightness after so many hours in the dark. "Finally, sunlight," she murmured.

"It makes no sense," Rick said. "There's no way we spent the whole night inside the grotto. It should still be night."

Julia checked her watch. It must have been damaged in the storm. "It's broken," she said.

Rick stared up at the grate. "The sun is high," he

noted. "It must be at least midday. I can't believe it. How could so much time have passed?"

"Forget it, Rick," Jason said. "We're here, we're safe. So what if the sun is shining?"

"Where do you guys reckon we are?" Julia asked.

Rick rubbed the back of his neck. "Best guess? I'd say we're somewhere under Salton Cliff, maybe on the other side of Argo Manor."

Jason began climbing the first step of the stairs. "No sense standing around," he commented.

"Yeah," Julia agreed, her legs leaden from the long night. "Let's go home."

Two voices, surprisingly close, stopped them in their tracks. Through the grate above, they heard two men in conversation.

"A shipment of the finest quality resin," the first voice said.

A deeper voice replied, "And has it already been sent to the market near the mastaba?"

"Naturally," the first voice replied. "But today it is almost impossible to move around. The pharaoh's guards are everywhere."

"Ah yes," the deeper voice said, "the pharaoh's visit. I will give my thanks a hundredfold if he stays away next time. Such a nuisance!"

The voices trailed off as they passed by the grate and continued on their way.

Rick and Julia exchanged a baffled look.

Rick quickly opened the *Dictionary of Forgotten Languages.* "Hold on, guys," he said. "I'm looking up 'mastaba'."

Up ahead, Jason stopped before a brick wall. He rapped his knuckles on it. "Another dead end," he groaned.

"Listen to this, guys," Rick said, reading from the book. *"A* mastaba *is a secret Egyptian tomb in the shape of a pyramid. The interior may be decorated with frescoes or engravings. On the outside, the entrance to the burial chamber is hidden in order to keep out grave-robbers."*

Julia looked puzzled. "Sacred Egyptian tomb? Burial chamber? Grave-robbers?" She suddenly whirled around to gaze at her brother, who was still probing the brick wall with his hands. "Jason!" she cried.

Rick slapped the dictionary shut. "He's in dreamland again," he said.

"Jason!" Julia repeated. "I know you better than any person alive. Are you hiding something from us?"

Jason turned to look at Julia and Rick. He was

just as astonished as they were. But there was a difference. He was bursting with joy.

"It worked," he told them, smiling. He thought back to the visions he'd experienced on the deck of the *Metis*, when the ship refused to move. How he'd suddenly known what to do. And how he'd wished with all his heart to travel to Egypt!

Rick stared at Jason. Then he looked at Julia, and at the strange new world in which they stood. And as he did, a knot formed in his stomach. He realized the bizarre, horrible, amazing truth. "We're not in Kilmore Cove any more," he said aloud. "This can't be Kilmore Cove."

"What do you mean, this isn't Kilmore Cove?" Julia said. She looked frantically from Rick to Jason. "What are you talking about?"

Rick pointed to the grate above their heads. "You heard those people. The resin, the *mastaba*, the pharaoh!"

Jason watched his friends intently. He still did not speak.

Julia wheeled around and glared at her brother. "Jason, you had better—"

"I had better . . . what, Julia?" Jason cut her off. He paused, the emotion welling up inside of him. "Don't you see?" he asked, his voice rising with excitement. "I took that ship through the storm. And do you know how? I imagined it! I hoped, I believed, and I wished it would take us here. Right here to this very spot."

He paused dramatically. "To Egypt."

Julia stood staring at her brother, bewildered.

Jason stepped forward. "Can't you see, Julia?" he said enthusiastically. "Ulysses Moore wanted us to come here. He left us clues and we followed them. He guided us to the place . . . to this *time*," Jason said.

Julia stepped away from her brother, closer to Rick.

"Now we have to decide," Jason said with conviction. "Do we keep going, or do we try to get back to Argo Manor?"

"Are you sure it's all that simple?" Rick said. He was still in a state of disbelief.

Jason wasn't listening. He gazed at the sunlight streaming in through the grate in the ceiling.

"Guys," he said. He placed one hand on each of their shoulders. "Listen to me. We're in Egypt! We can't turn back now," he urged. "Our destiny is here." He made a sweeping gesture with his arm. "Our destiny is awaiting us . . . out there!"

The adventure had just begun.

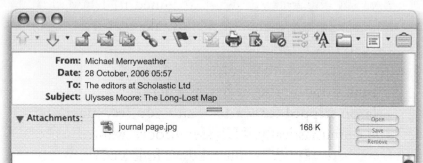

From: Michael Merryweather
Date: 28 October, 2006 05:57
To: The editors at Scholastic Ltd
Subject: Ulysses Moore: The Long-Lost Map

▼ Attachments:

| | journal page.jpg | 168 K | Open / Save / Remove |

I was right! I just found a loose page stuck to the bottom of the trunk. It looks like it's straight out of Ulysses Moore's manuscripts. From what I can tell, it's a drawing of an Egyptian building. Most interesting, though, is that the page has some writing on it. I've only been able to translate a few words, but I think it means "the long-lost map". I'm attaching a photo of it here.

What is the long-lost map? Could it be the title of Ulysses Moore's next manuscript? And what does this drawing mean? I'm going to find out, no matter what it takes. Please get the word out to everyone you can: there are more Ulysses Moore manuscripts out there.

I promise you this – the next time you hear from me, it will be when I've found and translated the rest of this manuscript. I won't rest until I have it.

Until then,
MM

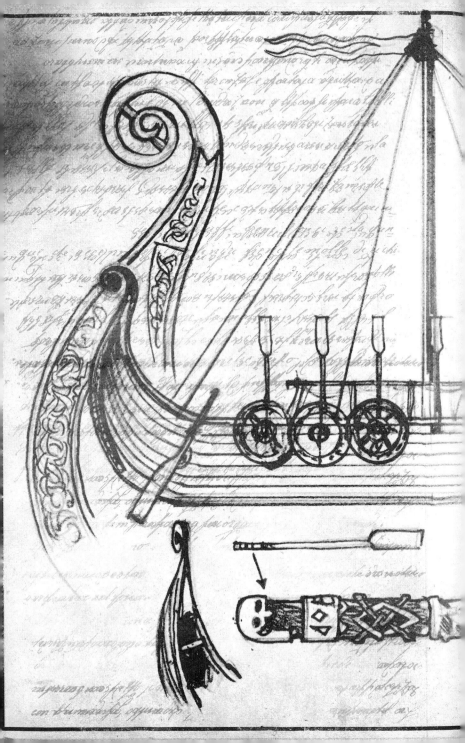

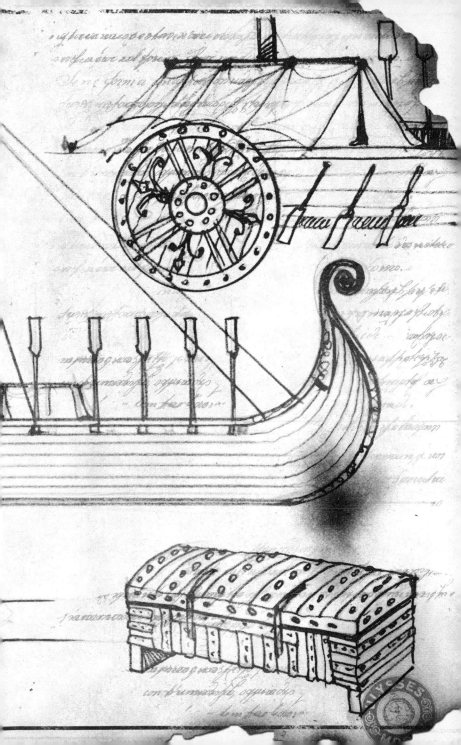

DON'T MISS BOOK TWO!

Ulysses Moore

ULYSSES MOORE

THE LONG-LOST MAP

The past is the key
to a secret. . .